"Why aren't you dating anyone?" Laura blurted, then wished that she could push the words back in.

But the widening of his eyes and the slight drop in his jaw said that there was no going back now. David had heard what was on her mind, and he looked…more than a little surprised. Well, she had lost some of her filter for saying what she was thinking over the past few months. Maybe it *was* the pregnancy hormones in action, or maybe it was simply the fact that she didn't understand the bizarreness of her old friend, her attractive and kind and nice—okay, a little more gorgeous than she remembered—old friend being *so* single.

When he didn't readily offer a response, Laura couldn't stand the silence. "Sorry, I was being nosy."

"Sometimes that's what friends do, right?" He leaned against the bookshelves and looked mighty nice doing it. "We are still friends, aren't we something else?"

Books by Renee Andrews

Love Inspired

Her Valentine Family
Healing Autumn's Heart
Picture Perfect Family
Love Reunited
Heart of a Rancher
Bride Wanted
Yuletide Twins

RENEE ANDREWS

spends a lot of time in the gym. No, she isn't working out. Her husband, a former all-American gymnast, co-owns ACE Cheer Company, an all-star cheerleading company. She is thankful the talented kids at the gym don't have a problem when she brings her laptop and writes while they sweat. When she isn't writing, she's typically traveling with her husband, bragging about their two sons or spoiling their bulldog.

Renee is a kidney donor and actively supports organ donation. She welcomes prayer requests and loves to hear from readers. Write to her at Renee@ReneeAndrews.com, visit her website at www.reneeandrews.com or check her out on Facebook or Twitter.

Yuletide Twins

Renee Andrews

Recycling programs for this product may not exist in your area.

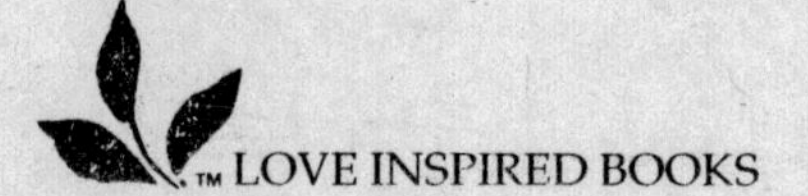

ISBN-13: 978-0-373-81729-0

YULETIDE TWINS

This edition published by arrangement with Love Inspired Books.

www.Harlequin.com

Printed in U.S.A.

Give, and it will be given to you. A good measure, pressed down, shaken together and running over, will be poured into your lap. For with the measure you use, it will be measured to you.

—*Luke* 6:38

This novel is dedicated to and inspired by
the precious twins I met 24 years ago,
Amber Gonzales Harrington and
Angel Gonzales Stroop. I've watched you grow into
young women with beautiful families of your own.
You've touched my heart and my life.

Chapter One

Laura Holland climbed out of her jam-packed Volkswagen bug and squinted toward the windows of the bookstore across the Claremont town square. During the entire four-hour drive from Nashville to this tiny North Alabama town, she'd attempted to convince herself that she'd made the right decision. Staying with her parents, especially with her mother threatening to leave again, was out of the question. But now she wondered what made her think she could show up here, reconnect with her old friend and somehow convince him to give her a job?

What if David sent her packing? Then where would she go?

Laura took a step toward the bookstore but halted when an elderly gentleman made his way to the entrance. He stood out from the other shoppers with his slow and steady gait. A shadow passed in front of the window as someone went to greet him when he entered.

Was that David? Laura remembered the tall, dark-haired guy who'd been Jared's college roommate the entire time he and Laura dated. Nice-looking in a Clark Kent kind of way, David wore dark-rimmed glasses, dressed impeccably and jogged regularly. He would be twenty-five now, merely two years older than Laura, and yet he'd already "made it" in the world, was self-sufficient and running his own business. A far cry from where Laura was now. More shadows passed in front of the awning-covered window, and then a man carrying a brief-case entered. How many people were in the store? And did she really want an audience when she begged for a job?

Spotting a rack of free classifieds outside of the five-and-dime, Laura grabbed a copy and sat on a wrought-iron bench while she waited for a few of David's customers to leave. If—and that was a big if—David was willing to hire her in her current state, she'd also need somewhere to live.

The unseasonable weather was nice enough that she could probably sit and browse the paper until dark. In Nashville, it'd already turned too cold to spend time outside. But here the first Monday in November felt uncommonly pleasant, with merely a slight chill in the air. Then again, Laura stayed warmer these days due to the extra weight she carried. She wondered if David was still the same big-hearted guy he'd been in college. Would he be willing to help her out? She suspected—and hoped—that he hadn't changed.

Laura rubbed her swollen belly. She sure had.

David Presley flipped the page of the quarterly report his accountant personally delivered and saw the nasty numbers on the P&L sheet identifying the sad state of his bookstore. He closed the folder, but the image of those red numbers wouldn't go away.

"I'll borrow more from my line of credit." The muscles in his neck immediately tightened, and he shifted his shoulders to relieve a little stress.

"Can I be honest with you, David?" Milton Stott had inherited the bookstore's account when his father retired, in much the same way David had inherited A Likely Story when his grandmother passed away. However, Milton's inheritance gave him the accounts of most everyone in town, so it wouldn't be all that terrible if he lost the bookstore as a client. David's inheritance, on the other hand, plopped all of his eggs in one basket. A basket that was, based on these numbers, almost empty.

Somehow David managed a smile. "I'd love to think that you weren't being honest and that those numbers were lying, but I know I can count on you giving me the truth. And since you've already delivered a painful dose, you might as well add the rest."

A noise in the back of the store caused Milton to turn. "You have a customer?"

David nodded. "Zeb Shackleford, but he wouldn't spread news of my financial state even if he heard it."

Milton heaved a sigh. "Okay, then. I'm going to tell it to you straight. Your grandmother barely got by with the store. I told Vesta she should sell the thing before she passed away so the family wouldn't be burdened. Your parents weren't interested in it...."

"They were pretty excited when Dad got the job opportunity in Florida." David's folks had been thrilled about the potential for a year-round warm climate, but even if they hadn't been tempted by the beach, they wouldn't have taken over running A Likely Story. They'd never appreciated the old store on the square the way he had.

"Well, Vesta knew they didn't want it and insisted you could breathe life into the old place. Back then, I told her that probably wasn't possible," Milton said, then added somberly, "I'm sorry that it appears I was right." He placed his copy of David's financials back in his briefcase and snapped it shut. "I don't see how you can keep the place open more than a couple of months, and that's only if you get enough holiday business to boost your numbers."

David swallowed past the bitterness creeping up his throat. He'd tried so hard to make the bookstore work, but Milton was right. He lost money every day the doors were open. He scanned the multitude of shelves lining the walls, the tiny reading corners his grandmother had insisted on having for customers to sit and enjoy their books—all of them persistently empty—and his sole customer, Zeb, gingerly perusing the packed shelves. "I'm not ready to give up," he told the accountant. "My grandmother thought I could make this place work, really believed it could be done, and that I was the one to do it. You said so."

"I also said that it probably wasn't possible," Milton reminded.

Zeb rounded the end of one of the stacks and held up his plastic basket. "Found some good ones today," he said with a grin.

David's heart moved with a glimmer of hope. "I had several bags of used books turned in this week for credit, so I thought you'd be able to find quite a few."

Zeb's face cracked into more wrinkles as his smile widened. Oddly, the weathered lines made him even more endearing. "Any of those suspense ones I've been looking for? Miss Tilly at the nursing home has been asking for some."

David pointed toward the other side of the store. "I think so. Look over there, about halfway down."

"Thanks." Zeb nodded at Milton. "Good to see you, Mil."

"You, too, Zeb." He waited for the old man to

move a little farther away, lowered his voice and said, "Credit? You're still taking books for credit? I told your grandmother years ago that she should stop that. It makes no business sense whatsoever."

"That's the way used bookstores typically work. And I carry new books, too, but there are folks in Claremont, like Zeb, who like the used ones." David said a silent prayer that Zeb would take his time finding the books he wanted so Milton wouldn't also learn the elderly man got his books for free.

Milton tsked and tapped David's folder on the counter. "Listen, I'm not charging you for my services this quarter. I know you can't afford it right now."

"I can't let you do that," David began, but Milton shook his head.

"Nope, not taking a penny. But what I *am* going to do is start praying that you'll think about what I've said and consider other options. You're a smart young man with a business degree from a great university and your whole life ahead of you. There are other things you can do, businesses that can make a profit and keep your head above water." Milton turned to leave. "However, if you're determined to give it a go, I'll pray for your success."

David agreed that a prayer wouldn't hurt.

Help me out, Lord. Show me what I need to do to breathe life into this place. I could really use some guidance here.

The bell on the front door sounded as Milton exited, and Zeb Shackleford edged his way toward David with books balancing over the top of his red plastic basket. He gingerly placed the basket on the counter and then reached to his back pocket and pulled out a worn leather wallet. "Now, I'm gonna pay you today, David. Please don't fight me on this. I got a lot of books, and I know you can't afford to keep giving 'em to me for free."

David suspected Zeb had gotten the gist of his conversation with Milton, even if he might not have caught every word. He loved the old man and the way he took care of so many people around Claremont. Right now he was trying to take care of David, but there was no way David would take his money. "We've been through this before. Those books are a donation."

Zeb opened the wallet and moved a shaky thumb across the top of a few dollar bills. "Please, David. Let me pay."

David placed his hand on top of Zeb's, and the trembling ceased. "It'd be different if you were keeping those books yourself, but I know that you'll be hauling them over to the nursing home and to the hospital and then to the shut-ins around town. You'll read the books to them, and then if they like the story, you'll let them keep them, won't you?" When Zeb didn't answer, David added, "My grandmother's last days were so much better because of your visits.

She loved listening to you read. You've got a way of bringing stories to life. She had that gift, too, before the cancer got the best of her. But with your visits, she could still enjoy a good story." He pointed to the books. "I'm not letting you pay for them."

"She never would take my money, either," Zeb huffed, folding the wallet and sliding it in his back pocket. Then he lifted his eyes and said, "I know you need the money."

David didn't want the older man to worry, even if his own anxiety made his stomach churn. He placed all of the man's books in two plastic bags. "I'll be fine."

Zeb placed a hand on David's forearm and squeezed. "You have a blessed day, son."

"I will." The words had barely left David's mouth when he heard someone moving through one of the aisles from the front of the store. He hadn't heard the bell sound, but he definitely had another customer. "Hello?"

Zeb turned so that he saw the pregnant woman at the same time as David. But David was certain Zeb didn't recognize the lady, since she wasn't from Claremont. David, however, did, and his heart squeezed in his chest the way it always had whenever he saw the stunning blonde in college. Infatuation had a way of doing that, lingering through the years, and David's had apparently hung around. "Laura?"

"Hey, David." She continued toward the counter.

"I came in when the other man left," she said, which explained why David didn't hear the bell, "and then I didn't want to interrupt you while you were talking to a customer."

"Well, I'm about to leave." Zeb extended a hand. "I'm Zebulon Shackleford, but folks around here call me Zeb."

"Laura Holland," she answered, shaking his hand and giving him a tender smile.

Holland. David didn't miss the fact that she was still Laura Holland. No married name. Why not? And who was the father of the baby she carried? So many questions, and he wanted to know the answers.

"I..." She hesitated. "I hope it's okay that I came here."

Shell-shocked, David realized he hadn't said anything more than her name. He mentally slapped himself out of the momentary stupor. "I'm sorry," he said. "Yes, of course it's okay." Though he suddenly wondered why she was here, in his bookstore, when he hadn't heard anything from her in over two years. The last time he'd seen her, in fact, she'd been very much in love with his college roommate.

Zeb slid his arms between the loops of the bags then pulled them off of the counter as he stepped away. "David, if it's okay with you, I might sit a spell and read in one of your nooks before I head out. I'm feeling a little weary and think it might do me good to rest a few minutes."

David had to forcibly move his gaze from Laura, still amazingly beautiful, to Zeb. "Sure, that's fine. And let me know if you want me to drive you home. It isn't a problem."

"Aw, I drove today, wasn't quite feeling up to walking this time. It's just that I parked on the other side of the square, and I think I'll handle that walk a little better if I sit a minute or two."

"Take all the time you need," he said, glad that his mind began to work again, the surprise of seeing Laura finally settling in to reality.

She looked even prettier than he remembered. She had her straight blond hair pulled back, drawing even more attention to pale blue eyes and a heart-shaped face. Jared had often compared her to Reese Witherspoon, and David agreed they were similar, but Laura was...Laura. Back then, he'd found an instant attraction toward the striking beauty, but as usual, he'd fallen into the role of second fiddle when she dubbed him her friend, and Jared her love. Then again, David was wise enough now to realize that his fascination with her had been merely that, a fascination. But beyond the intriguing element that'd always been a part of his relationship with Laura, had been the friendship that David had found with Jared's girl. He was certain that friendship was what brought her here now, because David knew she was no longer with Jared. His buddy had married in June.

Laura forced a smile, blinked a couple of times

and then seemed to struggle to focus on David, as though she were afraid if she looked directly at him, he'd see too much. Which was probably true.

In college, he mastered reading her eyes. If Jared had hurt her, David could see it in those telling eyes. He'd seen that look way too many times. Even though he was close to Jared, David never believed his old friend treated Laura the way she deserved. She had a kind heart and would do anything for anyone. Jared took advantage of that; he'd taken advantage of her love. David hated seeing that look of emotional pain in her eyes back then.

He studied her now and didn't see pain, but he saw something else that bothered him almost as much. Fear.

"Laura, is something wrong?" he asked, then quickly added, "I'm glad that you're here, but—" he decided it best to state the truth "—I haven't heard from you since I graduated from Tennessee, so to see you now, over two years later..." His gaze moved to her belly. "Do you need help?"

Her lip quivered, and then tears pushed free. She quickly brushed them away with two flicks of her hand. "I told myself I wouldn't cry."

David felt bad for causing her to release those tears, but he didn't know what else to say or do. However, he did know this—he would do whatever it took to help her. "Hey, it'll be okay." Rounding the counter, he did the only thing that seemed right—opened his arms and let her move inside his embrace. But he had no idea why she needed his comfort, so he said another silent prayer for God's guidance.

Laura let him hold her for a moment, but then he sensed her gaining her composure again, her shoulders rising as she sniffed then eased out of his hug. She looked up at him, and David suddenly felt taller than his six-one. He'd forgotten how petite she was, no more than five-four. Her size made him feel an even stronger urge to protect her from whatever had her so upset.

"I'm sorry I fell apart. I'll be okay." A lock of blond hair had escaped her barrette and rested along her cheek. She gently pushed it behind her ear. "It's been a long day."

David knew that was an understatement, but he'd maintain his patience and wait until she was ready to explain. He tried to think of what he could do to make her feel more comfortable. He had no idea where she'd parked or how far she'd walked to get to his store. Finding a spot at the square was sometimes difficult, so she could have walked a bit to get here, probably not all that easy with the pregnancy. "Why don't we sit and visit?" He pointed to the reading area nearest the counter. "I've got some lemonade in the kitchen. I'll get us a couple of glasses, and you can tell me what's going on."

She nodded. "Okay."

He went to the small kitchen in the back and poured two glasses of lemonade then returned to find her sitting in one of the oversize chairs pressing her hand against her belly and smiling.

"Here you go." He placed a glass on the table beside her and then took a seat on the sofa nearby. "Everything okay?" He indicated her hand, still rubbing against her stomach.

She nodded. "Yes, they get a little more active as it gets closer to night." A soft chuckle escaped when her hand actually edged out a little as something pushed—or kicked—from inside. "Makes sleeping quite a feat."

David would have said something about that kick, because he'd never seen anything like it, but instead he keyed in on the most important word in her statement. "They?"

Another nod, then she said, "Twins." She took a sip of the lemonade, swallowed and then announced, "Twin girls."

"Twin girls," he repeated, amazed.

Then, before he could ask anything like how far along she was, she added three words that put every question David may have had on hold.

"And they're Jared's."

He focused on her stomach. Twins were there. Jared's twins. His mind reeled at that. It'd been, what, over four months since he stood beside Jared as a groomsman at his wedding?

David continued staring at her swollen belly—he couldn't help it—and wondered how far along…

"Seven months," she whispered, obviously following his thought process. "I found out about the pregnancy the end of May, the week I graduated. By that time, our relationship had been over for two months, which was exactly how far along I was." She held the glass of lemonade, palms sliding up and down the clear column as her shaky voice continued. "I didn't know he'd been seeing Anita—seeing both of us—and then…he married her." Her attempted smile caused a couple of tears to fall free, and again she wiped them away. Then she seemed to gather the courage to tell him more and said, "He told me he'd pay to get rid of the baby." One shoulder lifted. "He had no idea there were two."

David's mouth opened, but no words came, and his opinion of his old roommate plummeted.

"My parents wanted me to put them up for adoption. They said it'd be better, you know, since I don't have a job or anything." She placed her glass on the table. "I got my early education degree, but schools aren't that interested in hiring a teacher who's going to have to miss work for doctor appointments and will be out for six weeks of maternity leave."

He tried to put the pieces together but still didn't see what had brought Laura here, to Claremont. However, he wanted to make sure that she knew, whatever she needed, he would try to help. "I hate it that you've had a hard time, and I'm really sorry that I haven't tried to contact you since I left." He'd thought of her often, but it didn't seem right calling Jared's girl, even after he knew they weren't together anymore. Plus he'd been seeing AnnElise Riley for the majority of that time, and she'd never have understood him reconnecting with an old, moreover attractive, female friend. Her jealousy had been over the top, which really made the fact that she'd cheated on David with her old boyfriend—and consequently left town with him—sting.

David shook away the bitter memory and concentrated on the woman in his bookstore. Now he wished he'd at least tried to check on her over the past couple of years.

"I didn't call you, either," she said softly, "so we're even."

That was true, but somehow it didn't help David's tinge of guilt. When Jared married Anita, he should have called to see if Laura was okay. And she was so not okay. She'd been several months pregnant when Anita walked down the aisle. David still couldn't get a handle on that fact. Why hadn't Jared at least mentioned it?

In any case, David would do what he'd always done back in college—help Laura after Jared had left her hurting. "Well, I'm glad that you've come here now, and I want you to know that if there's anything that I can do to help you, I will." He placed his glass next to hers then took her hands in his. "I mean that, Laura."

She blinked, nodded and then David saw pleading in those vivid blue eyes. "When my parents realized I wouldn't give up the babies and that I couldn't get a job in the school system, they offered to take care of everything. They wanted me to live with them, let them support me and the babies, for as long as I needed." One corner of her mouth lifted. "You remember how they were always fighting, how Mom was always threatening to leave or actually leaving. I didn't want my babies to grow up around that tension." Another sniff. "I want them to have a real home, somehow. And *I* want to take care of them."

David had met her parents a few times when they visited Laura in college. Her mother had always seemed angry or been pouting over one thing or another, and her father had tried to explain and make amends for her behavior. Laura had been even more independent because she didn't want to rely on them. "You didn't take them up on their offer."

She shook her head. "No, I couldn't. I've stayed with them the past few months, since I graduated, while I tried to find a job. At first I was able to substitute teach, but the schools don't even call me for that anymore. I think they're afraid I'll go into early labor." She gave him a soft smile. "Probably wouldn't be too great for my water to break in a classroom of first graders."

He grinned. "Yeah, probably not."

"But I want to show my folks that I'll be okay on my own. And I really didn't want to stay in Nashville." She touched her hand to her stomach, then added, "Jared and Anita live there."

David nodded. Jared and Anita were beginning their life in Laura's hometown, and he was certain she wouldn't want the slightest chance of running into her babies' father and his new bride.

"So, here goes." She took a deep breath, pushed it out. "I need a job. I want to support myself and my babies. And I thought of you and your bookstore, and—" she scanned the surplus of books "—I would work really hard for you. I know I'm limited physically now, but I can still sell books, and maybe I could help you start some reading programs or something like that? Something that would let me work with children, like I would have been able to do with my teaching degree?" She paused a beat then quietly added, "And I'll need help finding somewhere to live. I have a little cash in my savings, and I thought with this being a smaller town and all, maybe the cost of living would be lower than Nashville." She looked at him hopefully. "Do you think I could help you out? Or, I guess what I'm asking is, do you think you could help me out?"

He swallowed thickly through the lump lodging in his throat. He'd seen the worst figures ever this afternoon on his P&L statement, had even wondered how he'd stay in business past the holidays. Hiring someone wasn't something he'd have considered, at all. He couldn't pay himself, much less someone else. But this was Laura. And her baby girls. David knew the only answer he could give, even if it didn't make sense and even if it might give Milton Stott an early heart attack.

"Yes, I can use your help."

Chapter Two

Laura had been around David enough in college to know when something wasn't going right in his world. Right now, as he talked on the phone to the woman who owned the Claremont Bed-and-Breakfast, she could tell he wasn't getting the answer he wanted. He'd removed his glasses and placed them on the counter, then he pinched the bridge of his nose as he listened to what the lady had to say.

"No, Mrs. Tingle, I understand. I'd forgotten about the crafting folks coming in for the First Friday festival. They don't usually stay overnight, though, do they?" He flinched as she apparently delivered another bit of bad news, then his head slowly moved up and down. "That's right. I wasn't thinking about everything happening next week. Yes, the bookstore is going to offer some activities for the festival. I just haven't decided exactly what I'm doing yet." His jaw tensed. "Okay, I'll let Laura know you should have some rooms available in a couple of weeks."

Laura waited for him to look her way then mouthed, "No luck?"

He held up a palm and gave her a half smile in an apparent effort to let her know everything would be okay. But Laura's stomach quivered, and she began to think everything might not be okay. What if *every* room in town was booked for this festival he mentioned? For two weeks! Then what would she do?

"Yes, ma'am, we are having a book signing for Destiny Lee at the store next Saturday. That's the only thing I've officially set up so far, but it's definitely happening. It's her first signing and she's pretty excited about it." He nodded. "I'd heard she included a story about you and Mr. Tingle in the book. I look forward to reading it." He continued listening, then finally said, "That's okay, I'm sure we'll find something."

Laura didn't think he sounded so sure, and she wasn't feeling a whole lot of certainty, either. She waited for him to click the end button on his cell then asked, "Do you think all of the hotels in town are booked, too?"

He picked up his glasses and slid them back in place to rest on his nose. "See, that's the thing. Claremont doesn't *have* any hotels."

Laura felt her jaw drop. "None that have rooms, you mean?"

"None at all. The town's population is only 4,500. Usually the bed-and-breakfast offers more than enough room to house tourists...except when we have the crafting festivals."

"First Friday, that's a craft festival?" She'd heard him mention the term in his conversation.

"No, the First Friday festival happens every month, and it's basically a combination of crafters and performers, as well as a chance for all of the square's merchants to showcase their merchandise." He leaned against the counter. "First Friday brings in practically everyone from Claremont and the surrounding counties, but they don't typically stay overnight. However, November's First Friday is a little different, in that it leads into the annual Holiday Crafters Extravaganza, which lasts a full week. The crafters will have booths set up around the square through the following weekend, and each of the local stores coordinates activities for the festival, as well."

"And they've booked all of the rooms at the B and B," Laura said.

"As well as all of the hotel rooms in Stockville, which is the nearest city. Not that that would matter, though, since Stockville is a good twenty miles away, and you wouldn't want to drive that far." His brows lifted as he apparently thought of something, and then he asked, "About driving...how long will you be able to drive? I'm assuming there's a certain time when the doctors tell you to stop driving in pregnancy?" He glanced at her stomach and probably wondered how she could fit all of that behind the wheel. Laura had almost doubted the possibility herself, but she'd been able to pull it off by adjusting the steering wheel and seat.

"I don't have to stop driving," she said. "I did ask my doctor before taking the trip here today, not because I thought I couldn't drive but because I was traveling so far. She told me as long as I took periodic breaks to rest, I'd be fine, and I didn't have any problems." Laura had been amazed at how smoothly the trip had gone, but apparently the drive to Claremont wasn't her biggest dilemma. Thanks to the crafters in town, she had no place to stay. She'd been so worried about getting a job that she hadn't thought to consider locating a place to live before she traveled nearly four hundred miles. Her mother often said she acted too impulsively, and this was yet another time she'd be proving her right.

David must have noticed her anxiety because he moved to the seat next to hers and reached for her hand. The warmth of his large palm encircling hers reminded her of all the times he'd consoled her in college whenever Jared had let her down. Why couldn't her heart have fallen for someone like David instead of always tumbling head over heels for the one who'd treat her wrong? Even in high school, she'd been drawn to the bad boys. They just seemed so intriguing, dangerous and undeniably tempting.

"Some girls are just drawn to guys that treat them badly," her mother had said in an apparent effort to make Laura feel better about her situation. It didn't help. In fact, it only made her more resolute that she would *not* be hurt again, because she wasn't going to rely on a guy again.

Uh-huh, right. Then why did you come running here to David? her mind whispered.

Laura shook that thought away. She'd never thought of David "that" way. He was her friend and he'd always been there for her, just like he was now. This was a different situation entirely. She wasn't relying on a guy; she was counting on a friend.

"We'll find somewhere for you to stay," he said, solidifying the fact that she could, in fact, count on him. "Even if we don't find a place tonight, you have somewhere to go. You can stay in my apartment." He pointed to the ceiling. "It's above the bookstore."

Laura was touched that he'd offer, but she knew she couldn't accept. Asking David for help with the job was one thing; living in his apartment would be something different entirely. She'd gotten too close to Jared without the boundaries of marriage, and she'd been left to raise her babies on her own. She was certain *that* wasn't what David was offering, but still…the two of them staying together in his apartment wouldn't give the right impression to the people around town, or to David, for that matter.

She didn't need him thinking that she wanted

more. She didn't—not with David or with any guy. Not for a long, long time. The wound inflicted by Jared was still too raw. "David, I don't think that's a good idea, for us to stay together…." She searched for the right words but didn't have to say anything because David halted her progress.

"Oh, no—" he shook his head "—hey, that wasn't what I meant. *You* can stay in my apartment, and I'll stay with one of my friends in town."

She felt her cheeks flush. "Oh, I should have known that wasn't what you meant." A little surge of adrenaline, or something, pulsed through her veins as she tried to shake the embarrassment. She was seven months pregnant…with twins! "I'm sorry," she said, then added, "and embarrassed."

Still holding her hand, he tenderly squeezed her palm. "It's okay. A few years ago, those first three years of college, I'd have been exactly the kind of guy to ask a girl to stay at my place and wouldn't have thought a thing about it, but that's the old David."

His comment reminded her of the fact that he'd changed during his last year at UT. Something had happened that caused him to turn away from his wilder ways and back to his faith. Laura had been so wrapped up in Jared at the time that she hadn't thought a lot about what caused David's rapid transformation. But now she wished she could recall.

"So you don't have anything to worry about." He

grinned, and Laura spotted a slight dimple creasing his left cheek. Funny, she'd never noticed it before, but she liked it, very much. And she liked David, even more for making her feel at ease with her crazy presumption.

She laughed at her foolishness and slid her palm from his. For some reason, it suddenly seemed a little too intimate for their current relationship, friend-to-friend and boss-to-employee. "Okay, then, if you don't mind, and since there doesn't seem to be another place in town, I'll take you up on your offer."

The bell on the door sounded as someone entered the shop. "Welcome to A Likely Story," David called toward the front. Then he stood and held out a hand to help Laura rise from the chair.

She occasionally had a little trouble off-balancing her weight when she stood, and the support of his strong hand was a welcome addition. "Thanks."

"Anytime," he said, and she knew he meant it. David would help her stand and help her with a job and even help her find a place to live. Already, in less than an hour, he'd done more for her than anyone else had in years, and the gratitude for that compassion washed over her at once. She blinked back the urge to cry.

Luckily, a blond little boy dashed through the aisle knocking a few books from the endcap as he circled and taking Laura's attention off of herself and the man currently taking her under his wing.

"Kaden, please, slow down." A pretty brunette picked up the dislodged books and tucked them back in place then gave David an apologetic smile. "I told him we needed to hurry if we were going to make it to the bookstore before you closed at six, and I'm afraid he got the impression that we had to run all the way in."

"Not a problem at all," David said, tousling the boy's blond curls. "What ya so excited about, Kaden?"

"My teacher says I need some more books because I'm not—what did she say again, Mom?"

"Challenged," the lady said. "He's breezing through the sight word books and because of that, he's becoming a little disruptive during reading time at school."

"And we only get library day on Tuesday, and I can only check out one book for the whole entire week, and I really want more books than just one book, so Mom said we could come and buy some."

"I see," David said to Kaden.

Laura liked the way he didn't change his voice to talk to the boy. He spoke to him as though speaking to an adult, and Kaden nodded his head as if he totally believed David did see and understood his dilemma. Then he seemed to forget all about David as his attention zoned in on Laura. "Wow, how many babies are in *your* tummy?"

"Oh, my," his mother exclaimed. "Kaden, that isn't something that we ask..." She tapped her finger against her chin and seemed as though she didn't know how to complete her instruction to her son. Then she looked at Laura. "I'm so sorry. We have a baby at home—well, she's eighteen months now—but I had explained to Kaden when I was pregnant about how baby Mia was in my tummy. However, I forgot to explain how some women may not want to give the details…."

Kaden's brows drew together and he shrugged as though he couldn't figure out what he'd done wrong, and Laura laughed. "It's fine," she said. She pointed to her stomach and told Kaden, "Actually, there are two babies in my stomach. Two baby girls."

"Wow! Cool!"

This time David laughed, too, and Kaden's mother simply shook her head.

Kaden, undeterred, moved right on to his next pressing question. "So, can you help me find some books?" he asked, focused intently on David.

"Tell you what. This is my friend Miss Laura, and she just started working at the bookstore today." David tilted his head to Laura, and she smiled at Kaden, who turned his attention from David to her. "I think she will be able to help you find some really good books, and while she's helping you, I'm going to go get her things out of her car." He glanced to Laura. "Sound good?"

She felt a tinge of excitement at already being trusted to help a child. This was going to be…wonderful. "Sounds great." She'd dropped her purse on the table, so she turned, opened it and retrieved her keys. Handing them to David, she said, "It's the same Volkswagen I drove in school, and it's parked by the five-and-dime. I've got one large suitcase and a smaller makeup bag."

"That's it?" he asked.

"I brought some teaching supplies, just in case." She still hoped that she'd eventually get to teach. "But for now, I only need the two bags. I appreciate you getting them for me."

"No problem at all." David seemed to realize he'd forgotten introductions. "Mandy, this is Laura Holland. She's moved to Claremont and is going to be working here. Laura, this is Mandy Carter—Mandy Brantley, I mean. You'd think after all this time I'd get used to that."

"Not a problem," Mandy said.

"Mandy is married to the youth minister, Daniel Brantley, who also happens to be one of my best friends. And she owns Carter Photography on the square. She's a pretty amazing photographer. You'll have to check out her studio."

"Thanks," Mandy said. She smiled at Laura. "Nice to meet you."

"Nice to meet you, too."

"So, you ready to help me find books?" Kaden asked, grabbing Laura's hand and tugging her toward the children's area.

"Sure." Laura let him tug her away, but even

though she listened to Kaden talk about the kinds of books he liked, she also heard David ask Mandy whether he could bunk at their house tonight. Laura hated making David move out of his own apartment, but she didn't know what else to do.

"Which ones do you think I should try?" Kaden squinted at the titles on the shelves with his hands on his hips.

"Well, let's see." Laura scanned the books and was pleased with the variety David offered. "How about these Dr. Seuss books?"

"Already read 'em."

"All of them?" Laura asked.

He bobbed his head. "Yep."

"Here's a good one. *Where the Wild Things Are.*"

"Read it, too."

Mandy had finished talking with David and now walked to stand behind her son. "He loves to read."

"I can see that," Laura said, reaching for *Curious George's First Day of School.*

"I like Curious George, but I've read them already," Kaden said matter-of-factly. "But that one would be good for baby Mia." He pointed to the *Curious George Pat-A-Cake* board book.

"We'll get that one for her," Mandy said to Kaden, "but let's find some for you, too."

A hint of a memory crossed Laura's thoughts. David, talking about Mia from Claremont, and what a special person she was. But that wouldn't be this baby, since she hadn't even been born at the time. Laura tried to remember, but before she could bring the memory into focus, Kaden forged ahead in his search for books.

"What else do you have, Miss Laura?"

Laura ran a finger along the spines and then saw a group that she thought might appeal to Kaden, if he hadn't read them yet. She pulled out the first book in the series. "How about *The Boxcar Children*? Those were some of my favorite books when I was young."

"Mine, too," Mandy said.

Kaden took the book and studied the illustration of four children and a red boxcar on the cover. "Is it a girl book, or is it for boys, too?"

"It's a great book for both boys and girls," Laura said.

"That's true," Mandy agreed. "Our librarian, Miss Ivey, read the books to us when I was in elementary school. Everyone loved them, and then we'd go on the playground and pretend we were the boxcar children."

"What's it about?" Kaden asked.

Laura could tell his interest was piqued. "It's about four brothers and sisters who have run away and find a boxcar to live in."

"They have to take care of themselves? All by themselves?" Kaden asked.

"Yes, they do. And there are all of these books that tell you about their adventures."

"Okay, I want some of these books, Mom! I wonder if Nathan knows about them. He might like them, too, huh?"

"Nathan is one of Kaden's older friends," Mandy explained.

"He's nine," Kaden said.

Laura thought about the possibility of Kaden and his friends starting to read the series together. That could be a very good thing, not only for the kids, but also for her to prove herself as an asset to David's bookstore. "Why don't you see if Nathan, and maybe some of your other friends, would like to read the stories? I'm sure Mr. David would be happy to order more copies, and then all of you could read them together." Her mind kept churning, and she liked where her ideas were headed. "Maybe we could start a *Boxcar Children* club here, and you could all come talk about the books and the adventures."

David entered the children's area a little winded from his trek with the luggage, but he'd obviously heard Laura's idea. "That sounds good to me," he said.

"I've never thought about a book club for children, but given Kaden's appetite for reading, it'd be great for him. I'll call Nathan's parents tonight, as well as a few more of Kaden's friends," Mandy said. "Go ahead and get the first three books in the series, and we'll get that board book for Mia."

"How is the littlest Brantley?" David asked.

"Chattering up a storm now," Mandy said. "I'll bring her the next time I come."

"Sounds great," he said, then to Laura added, "I got your luggage. I put it by the checkout counter for now, but I'll carry it upstairs for you after Mandy and Kaden are done shopping."

"We're ready," Kaden said, grabbing the three books and clutching them to his chest. "I want to go read some before I have to go to bed."

"Okay, take the books up to the counter so we can pay," Mandy instructed, and Kaden ran off with his new books. Then she turned to David. "Daniel and I would love for you to stay with us, but I think I have a better idea. My apartment is open above my studio. I haven't lived there since Daniel and I married three years ago, but I kept the furnishings intact. Laura, you could stay there. It's clean and ready, and you could stay as long as you like."

"Oh, I couldn't take advantage of you that way," Laura said.

"Nonsense. It's just sitting there, and it'd be convenient for you if you're working at the bookstore. It's only a few doors down on the square. And then David wouldn't have to stay anywhere else, either. It'd be perfect."

"I'd want to pay you," Laura said.

"We'll work something out," Mandy promised. "I'll ask Daniel about payment, but really, we haven't been using it anyway."

"That would be convenient," David said, "if it sounds good to you, Laura."

"It sounds great, actually. Thank you, Mandy." She was a little stunned that someone she just met would offer her a place to stay, but she could already tell, not only from David, but also by the first people she met in Claremont, that people here were different, and she meant that in a very good way. Maybe, in Claremont, she and her babies would have a real home.

Chapter Three

David used the key Mandy gave them to unlock the door to her studio, then carried Laura's luggage through the gallery and toward the apartment. "All of the shops on the square are designed the same, with a kitchen in the back and then a small second-floor apartment. My grandparents lived above the bookstore when they first started out, but then they bought a farmhouse a little ways out from town when they had my mother."

He'd reached the kitchen and turned to make sure Laura was doing okay, but she wasn't there. Instead, she'd stopped to admire one of Mandy's photographs displayed on an easel. David put the luggage down and went to see what had her attention.

The photo was of Mandy, very pregnant, wearing a white dress with her hands cradling her stomach. Kaden and Daniel were on either side of her with their hands placed against hers and also appearing to cradle the new addition to their family.

Laura's hand was at her throat, her eyes glistening at the image. "It's beautiful, isn't it?" she whispered.

David swallowed, uncertain whether she was talking about the photo itself or the beauty of a complete family, something she didn't have for her little girls. His heart ached for her, and he longed to reach out and hold her, but he didn't want to make her uncomfortable. She'd balked earlier when he said she could stay in his apartment because she thought he was trying to cross the line into a personal relationship. But David had determined long ago that his relationship with Laura was strictly friendship. And right now she needed a friend.

"You're going to be a great mother, Laura. And your relationship with your girls will be beautiful, too," he said honestly.

She blinked a couple of times, moved her eyes from the photograph to David, and undeniable gratitude shone from the pale blue. "You think so, David? Really?"

He realized that she needed reassurance of the fact and that she probably hadn't received it from anyone else. Jared had asked her to end the pregnancy, and her parents practically begged her to put the babies up for adoption. But Laura wanted her girls, and David needed her to know that he believed in her. A single tear leaked from her right eye, and he placed a finger against the droplet on her cheek to softly wipe it away. "I know so," he said. "Just think about what you did tonight, talking with Kaden and helping him get excited about reading and sharing his books with his friends. You're a natural."

"He's six," she said, "a bit different than newborns, don't you think?"

"Motherhood instincts *are* there, and you *are* a natural. Like I said, you're going to be great, and they're going to love you."

She studied the photo another moment then said, "Thanks. I really needed to hear that."

"You're welcome. Now let's go get you settled in."

This time she followed him through the gallery. He picked up the luggage when they reached the kitchen and then stopped at the foot of the stairs. "You go first, and I'll follow."

She gave him a knowing glance. "You afraid I'll get off balance and fall? I'll have you know I've had to tackle some form of stairs nearly every day of the pregnancy, and they haven't gotten the best of me yet. And now that I'll be living here, I'll navigate these every day."

"Yeah," David said, eyeing the steepness of the stairwell. "And I'm not so sure that's a great thing. Maybe we should keep looking for other rental places, some that are on the first floor."

She smirked. "Never knew you to be such a worrier. I can still drive—the doctor said so—and I can still climb stairs." She stepped ahead and started up the first steps. "But if it will make you feel better,

I always use the handrails." She placed a firm palm on the banister to prove her point. "See?"

"Yeah, I see," he said, but he still wasn't thrilled at the thought of her climbing all of the stairs every day. What if she did fall? More worries came to mind. What if she went into labor trying to make her way to the apartment? Or what if she went into labor in the apartment and then had to climb down the stairs to get to the hospital? As if he wanted to make certain she knew, he said, "When you go into labor, just call me. I'll make sure you get to the hospital in time."

Her smirk moved into a smile. "You're precious, you know that?"

"Precious, yep, that's me. *That's* what I go for." And that's what he'd always been to Laura, and to most every other girl before the relationships eventually ended. Precious. A friend.

She laughed, and even though he wasn't thrilled with his never-changing "best bud" status, he was glad to have given her that luxury. "You know what I mean," she said.

"Yeah, I do." It was the same thing Mia Carter had meant when she told him she'd fallen for Jacob Brantley. And then AnnElise Riley last year, when she'd left town with Gage Sommers. And, the most memorable of all, Laura herself, who'd fallen for his college roommate without even realizing David was captivated, as well.

And although David had experienced one semi-long-term relationship in college with a girl who did, in fact, think he hung the moon, he'd ended the relationship with Cassadee because she hadn't shared his faith.

And *that* was what David wanted—the kind of relationship that lasted for life, with God in its center—what he'd witnessed with his grandparents and parents. He'd never felt *that* toward Cassadee, or Laura, or any of the others, really. But he had no doubt he would, one day, in God's time. For now, though, he'd be a friend to the cute, very pregnant woman making her way up the stairs.

Laura slowed her progress as she examined several photographs. In the gallery, the only personal photo of Mandy's was the one Laura had noticed; however, all of the photos lining the stairwell were of Mandy's family. "Is that Mandy's husband?" She pointed to a photo of Mandy, Daniel and Kaden amid a group of children in Africa.

"Yes, they lead up a support effort in Malawi that our church funds, and they travel down every other year to check on the kids."

"That's so wonderful," she whispered, then took another couple of steps before she stopped again, her head tilting at the largest photo on the wall. "That's Kaden, right?" She pointed to the toddler between the couple. "And that's Mandy's husband, but that isn't Mandy, is it?"

David's chest caught a little when he looked at the image, the way it always did when he remembered his dear friends. "Actually, that isn't Daniel. It's his twin, Jacob. And that's Mandy's sister, Mia. They're Kaden's parents, but…"

Laura audibly inhaled. "I remember now. Mia, that was your friend you were so close to from home, and during your senior year at UT they were killed in a car accident."

"Hit by a drunk driver," David said, that painful memory slamming him the way it always did. "Kaden was only three, and Mandy adopted him."

"And Daniel?" she asked, glancing between the two pictures to see the powerful resemblance between the identical twins.

"He'd been serving as a full-time missionary in Africa, at the place the church supports, but came back to help Mandy raise Kaden."

"And they fell in love," Laura said, emotion flowing through her words. "What a sad—and beautiful—story."

David nodded, his own emotions not allowing him to say more. Then he cleared his throat and forced his attention away from the photos. "You want to head on up? The luggage is getting a little heavy here." David winced at the lie. He hadn't intended to tell it, but he hadn't expected to reminisce over painful memories tonight, either.

Laura gave him a look that said she knew he

wasn't telling the truth but that she'd also let it go. Evidently she knew he was tired of thinking about Jacob's and Mia's deaths. "Sorry," she said softly, then completed the few steps left to reach the apartment.

She glanced in the first bedroom, a twin bed against one wall and bookshelves lining the remainder of the room. A baseball comforter covered the bed, and a long blue pillow with *Kaden* embroidered in red centered the headboard made of baseball bats. "Oh, how cute!" she said, taking it all in. "I want to have a neat room for my girls, too. I need to start thinking about that."

"Well, from what Mandy has told me, Kaden has an identical room to that one at their home. When she and Daniel married, they were going to move all of Kaden's things to the new place, but then Mandy said she knew he'd be spending a lot of time here with her, especially in the summer when school is out, so she kept his room intact. She also converted one of her studio rooms downstairs into a room for Mia."

"See, that's the thing that would be great about being a teacher. I could have my summers off to spend with the girls," Laura said. "I'll look at the room she did for Mia later. Maybe I can get some ideas for my girls. I want their room to be special, like this one is for Kaden."

"I've got some magazines at the bookstore that

should help you out. I get several home design ones for the moms in town, some specifically for decorating children's rooms."

"That'd be great," she said, but her tone wasn't overly enthusiastic. Before David could ask why, she added, "Mandy said this apartment has two bedrooms. And I'm sure she won't want me changing things, since this is obviously Kaden's room."

David understood. She wanted a special place for her girls, and she wouldn't be able to decorate for them here, unless Mandy and Daniel allowed this to be something fairly permanent. David suspected they would offer, but he didn't know if that's what Laura wanted. "She has several studio rooms downstairs, and I don't think she uses them all. She may let you change one of them."

"Yeah," she said, "but still, I hope that eventually I'll have something more like—" she paused, swallowed "—a home." Then she looked to David and shook her head. "I'm sure that sounded like I'm not grateful Mandy gave me this place to stay, or rather is going to let me rent it. I *am* going to pay rent." She frowned. "I didn't ask what you'd pay me at the bookstore, and anything will be fine—I promise—but you'd know more than I do.... Will I be able to afford the rent here?"

David wished he could pay her what a college graduate deserved, but he wasn't sure how he was going to pay her at all. "I think Daniel and Mandy will give you a very reasonable rate." Of that he was certain, and whatever that rate was, David would make sure he gave her enough hours and enough pay for her to live here. Somehow. And he didn't want to worry about that anymore now. But the look on her face said she was uncertain, and she had enough on her plate without having to be concerned over how to pay her rent. "You'll be able to pay it." He smiled, and thankfully, she did, too.

"Well, let's go see the other rooms." She left Kaden's room and continued past a small bathroom and into a larger bedroom. "Oh, this is so nice."

David followed her into the room and placed the larger piece of luggage on the floor and her makeup bag on the dresser. The bed was an antique, beautifully carved and cloaked in a handmade quilt. Embroidered circular doilies decorated each nightstand with antique lamps in the center. Long, slender embroidered linen covered the dresser. And, looking a bit out of place amid the furnishings, a small flat-screen television topped a highboy chest of drawers. "You like it?"

Laura ran her hand along the bumpy quilt and smiled. "I love it. Granted, it may not be a permanent home for me and the babies, but it's a beautiful place to start, isn't it?"

"Yes, it is."

Like the remainder of the apartment, the room had an abundance of photographs on the walls, all of these black-and-white images, some landscapes and additional family photos. Laura spotted a framed photo at one end of the dresser. She picked it up and studied the image of Mandy and Mia, the two girls hugging tightly and smiling from ear to ear. "They were really close, weren't they?"

David blinked, nodded. "Yeah, they were."

"I hope my girls are that close, too." She kept looking at the picture, then glanced up at David, and her voice was barely above a whisper when she asked, "You loved Mia, didn't you?"

He honestly couldn't remember how much he'd shared with Laura that night at UT when he'd gotten the call that informed him Mia was gone. Maybe she already knew the answer. But even so, he wouldn't lie to her about it. "I was pretty sure I loved her in high school, you know, young love and all of that. I thought I'd marry her," he admitted. "But she was two years behind me in school, and when I left, she kept hanging around with all of our friends, and she and Jacob fell in love." David thought it was important to add, "And I was happy for them. Maybe not at first, but after I saw how much they meant to each other, and how happy Mia was, I *was* happy for them."

Laura's head moved subtly, as though she were putting the pieces together. "So those first years at UT, when I met you and you were dating so much and partying so much, you were trying to get over her."

It wasn't a question, so David didn't answer. There was no need. It was the truth. Except he wouldn't add that he would've dated Laura if she'd have looked at him the way she looked at Jared.

"And then, when she died, that's when you changed." Her head nodded more certainly now, as though she had no doubt whatsoever in the truth of her statement. "You turned to your faith after you lost your friends. I remember that. No more partying, no more dating everyone on campus."

David fought the impulse to tell her that the only girl he'd ever really wanted to date at UT was the one standing in this room. Instead, he said, "I realized I hadn't had any peace without my faith. And when I needed something to hold on to, something real, that's where I turned."

"I remember that," she said, placing the photo back on the dresser and turning toward David. "You found God, about the same time that I lost Him."

Her mouth flattened, and David sensed the sadness in her admission. Back in college, every now and then, particularly when she was upset, he'd had intense conversations with Laura, the kind where you wonder if you said too much, opened up too much, showed your pain too much. Then he would hold her until she was okay. He moved toward her with the intention of holding her again, but she stepped back and shook her head.

"I'll be okay," she said. "It's like that saying, if you find yourself farther from God, who moved?" She waited a beat and then whispered, "I did."

In spite of all the tough conversations David had with Laura before, he'd never said anything about faith, or God. At the time, that wasn't at the top of his priorities. Now, though, it was. "Laura, we have an amazing church here, full of people who understand God's love and His grace. Why don't you come with me Wednesday night for the midweek worship?"

The look she gave David resembled shock. Then she glanced down at her stomach and shook her head. "Trust me, I have no business in church right now."

"Laura—" he began, but she cleared her throat.

"Please, David. I don't want to talk about it. I just want to get my things unpacked and relax awhile. It's been a long day."

David knew when a conversation had been ended, and this one was done, in spite of how important he felt it was for her to find her faith again, for her to find the peace that he'd found again. "Sure," he said and turned to go, but he wasn't giving up. He'd already determined several ways he hoped to help Laura. He wanted to help her support her babies until she was able to get a teaching job, and he'd do that—somehow—at the bookstore. And he wanted to help her find her faith and the peace he'd experienced again since he'd turned his life back over to God. In other words, David wanted to help her have the two things she needed most—a friend and a Savior.

Chapter Four

"What's that you're working on?" Zeb Shackleford peered over Laura's shoulder at her pitiful sketch.

"We're starting a book club for kids," she said. "The first series we're reading is *The Boxcar Children.* I thought it'd be nice to decorate the children's area to look like a boxcar." She frowned at the plain red rectangle on the page. "I was going to do a sketch and then go to the craft store to see what materials I could use to create a big prop." She shook her head again at the image on the paper. "But my artistic skills are rather lacking."

He set the two books he'd been holding on a table nearby and gingerly lowered himself into the seat next to hers. "You know, my sweet Dolly used to say I had quite a knack with a pencil and paper. I used to draw all of the scenes for her classroom bulletin boards. You want me to give it a go for you?"

"Would you mind?" Laura gladly relinquished the sketch pad and colored pencils to the kind man.

"I'd be honored." He turned the page to a clean sheet, opened the box of pencils and selected the charcoal one. Laura had propped *The Boxcar Children* book on the table to use as a go-by, and he squinted at it for a few seconds then began to draw. It didn't take but a minute of watching him move the pencil around the page for Laura to see that he really did have a talent.

"Dolly," she said as he drew, "is she your wife?"

"For fifty-seven years before the Lord called her home." He paused, looked at Laura and said, "I'm looking forward to seeing her again."

Touched by the affection in his tone, Laura didn't know what to say. She'd met Zeb Monday, only four days ago, but already she'd grown very attached to the kindhearted man who visited the store each day.

"She was a teacher, too," Zeb said, then turned his attention back to sketching.

"I'm not a teacher yet." She'd talked to Zeb about her dream to become a teacher, as well as how she'd had to put that plan on hold until she had her babies and until schools were willing to hire her.

Zeb completed the boxcar—which looked amazing—and began to draw the children from the book cover. Laura didn't really need the children drawn, since she was only planning to design a big boxcar prop, but he was doing such an incredible job that she didn't want to stop him. "You know," he said, "the way I see it, teaching doesn't have to occur inside school walls." He pointed to the book. "Sounds like you're already working toward encouraging some of the kids around here to increase their joy of reading. That's teaching, any way you look at it."

Laura smiled. She *had* felt good about the responses they'd already received for the book club. "I guess it is." Several of Kaden's friends had signed up, and she anticipated adding more tonight if she got this display done and could advertise it properly for the First Friday event. "I've decided to hold the Boxcar Book Club gathering each Monday after school. I thought that'd be a good way to start each child's week, and I'm planning to bring in some of the activities from the book to make it more interactive."

"Dolly did the same thing, tried to give the kids more hands-on activities when they were learning. She said it helped them retain what they learned if they had an action associated with it." He put down the pencil and turned the page toward Laura. "I think she'd have liked this. Do you?"

The detail of the boxcar, as well as the four children, was astounding. "It's incredible."

"Okay, so to create this to scale, I believe you'll need six pieces of craft board, the thickest kind they sell. You'll also need to fix this door so it opens, because they'll probably want to go inside of it, don't you think?"

Laura nodded. "That's what I wanted."

He ran tiny dashes around the drawing to show how he believed the boards should be assembled. "Then all you'll need is some wood stands to hold it in place. I'm pretty sure David can get wood for you out of some of those crates that are always stacked behind the stores."

He handed her the sketch pad. "Take it over to Scraps and Crafts. It's straight across the square—you can't miss it. Diane Marsh owns the place and will be able to tell you exactly what you need to build a boxcar prop for the kids." He lifted a finger. "Her grandson is about Kaden's age. Have you got an Andy Marsh on your list of kids signed up?"

Laura remembered the name. "Yes, I do."

"Chances are, Diane will donate the materials if she knows it'll help Andy enjoy his reading. She's talked to me about that before, wanting him to learn to like books."

"I'm pretty sure it was his grandmother who called and signed him up," she said.

Zeb grinned. "Sounds like Diane. She loves those grandchildren. The other ones are older, teens I think. If you start something for teens, she'll probably sign them up, too."

Laura had been thinking the same thing, that if

this book club was a success, she could start more. "I hope to do just that."

He pushed up from the chair and picked up the two books. Glancing at his watch, he said, "I'd go with you to see Diane, but I'm supposed to be at the hospital in a half hour so I'd better go."

"The hospital?"

"I read to the kids on the children's floor a couple of days each week during their lunch." He turned the books so Laura could see the titles, *Daniel and the Lion's Den* and *The Story of Moses*. "Picked a couple of Bible stories for today."

Laura's heart moved the way it did every time she heard about one of Zeb's regular activities. She'd never met anyone like him. "That's wonderful, Zeb. I'm sure they love having you read to them."

He leaned one of the books toward Laura and said, "You should go with me sometime, and David, too. I've got to tell you, they do way more for me than I do for them. Makes you really understand what Christ meant when He said it's more blessed to give than to receive, you know?"

Laura nodded. She did know, and yet that made her current situation all the more painful. David had asked her to go to his midweek Bible study on Wednesday at the Claremont Community Church, and she'd declined. And Mandy had invited her to a ladies' Bible study that she was hosting last night, and again, she'd declined. Now Zeb was reminding her subtly that…she missed church. But she'd so blatantly turned her back on God that she wasn't certain He'd want her. And she didn't know whether she could handle the guilt of entering a church and being surrounded by all of the people who "got it right."

Zeb had turned his attention to the two children's books in his hand and didn't notice Laura's discomposure. Instead, he flipped through the pages and smiled. "These illustrations are beautiful. The kids will love them." He moved toward the counter. "I'll leave the money over here so you don't have to get up."

"Don't leave any money, Mr. Zeb. David doesn't want you to pay, and neither do I. And I'm getting up anyway." She maneuvered her way out of the chair, then winced when one of the babies apparently kicked her for disturbing her sleep. "Whoa."

He quickly turned from the counter. "You okay?"

"Yes," she said, gritting her teeth as another kick matched the first, then exhaling when the twins finally settled down. "I'm fine. One of them is apparently attempting to teach the other one karate," she said with a laugh. "But I'm not taking your money."

He frowned. "I told you not to get up."

"I'm going to the craft store as soon as David gets back from the post office, so I needed to get up anyway. And I want to walk you to the door." She gently steered him farther away from the checkout counter and toward the door.

"You're just trying to keep me from paying."

"And I'm doing a pretty good job of it, too, aren't I?" She smiled, gave him a hug and then opened the door for him to leave.

"One of these days I'm going to repay you," he said.

"You can repay me by letting me go with you to visit those kids one day. That sounds like a teacher's dream."

He smiled. "It is. You have a blessed day, Miss Laura."

"You, too."

Zeb exited, leaving Laura alone in the bookstore. That was something she'd noticed this week more than anything else; it was almost always empty. In the four days she'd been working, Laura had learned how to collect used books and log the credits in the computer, how to shelve the titles according to genre and author, how to select which books would appeal to readers in the various reading nooks and how to guide customers in their purchases. All of that could be considered part of her job description, but it wasn't the most important thing she learned during her first week on the job.

She learned David wasn't making any money.

Throughout the week, they'd received several bags of used books from customers who typically swapped out for other books during the same shopping trip. Then they had a few who came in and visited, browsed titles and perhaps even sat in a reading nook to peruse a book for a while before they placed it back on the shelf. Hence, no revenue. And while David did offer a few new books for purchase, the majority of the store was composed of trade-ins, and most of his sales were for credit. Or, in the case of Zeb Shackleford, free.

Laura didn't mind David giving so many books to the precious older man, but she didn't understand how he could continue running this business with virtually no income. And then this morning he'd given her a paycheck for her first week of employment, and he'd paid her well. Nothing excessive, but more than she'd expected considering the fact that he let her rest whenever she needed, let her go to her doctor's appointment yesterday and told her she could arrive late and leave early if she felt weary from the pregnancy.

But with the lack of customers and income that Laura had seen this week, she had no doubt David wasn't making enough money to support the store, much less to pay Laura as though everything were a-okay, hunky-dory.

And something else that wasn't a-okay or hunky-dory was the fact that her good-looking and nice guy of a boss was undeniably single. She'd paid attention throughout the week; he never texted, didn't phone anyone for quiet conversations, and even though several pretty ladies had stopped by the store over the past few days, he'd offered nothing more than a friendly smile. No flirting. No invitations for dinner or even coffee. And Laura got the impression that at least a couple of the twentysomething females had stopped by specifically to see the dashing owner and maybe even find themselves on the receiving end of his attention.

But David didn't appear to even notice he had a following. Then again, Laura had never actually realized how cute he was until this week. Maybe it was the pregnancy hormones kicking in. Or maybe he'd always been attractive, and she'd been too absorbed in Jared to notice. But in any case, he hadn't seemed the least bit interested in any of the single ladies of Claremont, which was a problem. A big one. Because Laura needed him to be interested in someone else. That would control this ridiculous notion that he might be interested in the very pregnant friend working in his shop. And it would also control her bizarre impulse to return the interest. Ever since their heart-to-heart Monday night, when he talked to her about loving and losing Mia, she'd felt even closer to David. And she wasn't ready for a relationship, at all.

Merely thinking about that day when she realized that she was pregnant and when Jared practically demanded that she end the pregnancy caused Laura's stomach to pitch. She'd jumped into that relationship headfirst and had been undeniably stupid. She wouldn't make that mistake again. Oh, no, it would be a long time before she handed her heart over. But when she did, she knew what she wanted. A guy who was honest. A guy who was faithful. A guy who loved her completely—no one else, just Laura—and a guy who she loved the very same way.

She flinched as an image of David carrying her luggage up the stairs overtook her thoughts. David, giving her a job. David, holding her hand to help her stand. That was the kind of guy she wanted next time, but she simply wasn't ready for that yet. Not that it mattered. There was still the fact that she'd dated his friend, was having his babies, in fact. And the fact that she didn't exactly look the part of a girl anyone would date, seven months pregnant and waddling. And, as far as David was concerned, she didn't share his faith. Not anymore. She'd given up on God because she assumed He'd given up on her.

Plenty of reasons for David not to look at her beyond friendship. Which was good. Exactly what she wanted.

Really.

The bell on the front door rang, and Laura turned to see the object of her thoughts entering with a big brown box tucked under one arm. He wore a black cashmere sweater over a blue-and-white striped button-down shirt, well-worn jeans and black boots. He scanned the store. "No customers?"

She shook her head then tucked a wayward lock of

hair behind her ear. In spite of all of the cute maternity clothes her mother had bought her for the pregnancy, she never felt like she looked half as good as he did. Because right now, he looked very good. She stopped herself from attempting to check her reflection in the nearest window and tried to control the nervousness that had started occurring whenever her boss came around. "It's been a slow hour," she said. Truthfully, it'd been a slow week, but she wouldn't point out the obvious.

"That's okay. It'll give us time to check out what we got in the mail." A dark wave of brown hair shifted to cover one eye as he nudged the door shut with his shoulder. He jerked his head to the side to toss it back into place. Laura liked the way he managed to dress neat but also look rumpled, like he'd taken in a game of Frisbee on the square on his way to the post office. In college, he'd often played ultimate Frisbee with Jared and several of the other guys they hung around. Even though David gave the appearance of being Mr. Studious, he'd surprised everyone with his athleticism and competitiveness on the quad. Laura had thought it funny that he'd turned out to be the superb athlete in the bunch, something Jared and the gang hadn't expected.

Funny…and impressive.

She shook the memory of David running and diving for those soaring discs and told herself she would stop recalling anything about him that might be considered overly appealing. He was appealing enough without being an athlete, too. But this was a business relationship between friends. He'd given her a job and helped her find a place to stay, and he'd watched over her since she arrived in Claremont like any good friend would do. So this emotion that kept creeping in was gratitude. That was it, gratitude. And she had to keep reminding herself of that fact.

"The *Boxcar* books came in today. I got a case, forty-eight books. You really think we might have that many kids show up?"

Laura had asked him to get the books Tuesday morning, before she realized that the bookstore didn't appear to hold its own moneywise. Now she feared if she didn't have that many kids to purchase those books, she'd end up costing him more than she made. She swallowed. David had helped her too much for her to hurt his business, so she *would* make this work; she had to. "Sure we will," she said, and did her best to sound upbeat, enthusiastic, excited even.

His smile said he bought it, and Laura breathed a sigh of relief. If David was right and the majority of the town showed up tonight for the First Friday event, she'd focus on finding kids to join that club… and selling their parents the book. David might not have had the time to figure out ways to make money for himself and his store, but Laura wasn't about to work here and not offer some sort of appreciation for the deal. And her appreciation would come in the form of more customers for her boss.

"You do realize that there's no way we could handle forty-eight kids in the children's area at once. I'd say we couldn't seat more than fifteen at the most," he said.

Laura hadn't thought about that, but he had a point. And if she sold all of those books, she'd need to make sure she had room for all of the kids. "What if we had the book club each day after school instead of only on Mondays?" She remembered what Zeb said about potentially starting a teen book club, too. "And if we did additional book clubs for teens or adults, we could put those later in the day."

"You're counting on this taking off, aren't you?" he asked.

"I am," she admitted. "It'd be a good thing for the store, wouldn't it?"

"Definitely a good thing." He picked up the list of kids who had already signed up for the book club. "Nine so far." His mouth slid to the side as he silently read the names. "I know all of these kids, and some of them aren't even close in age. Nathan and Autumn are both nine, maybe ten. And Kaden, Abi and Andy are all younger, six or seven, I'd say. Do you think we should divide them up by age?"

"That's a good idea," Laura said. "I'll call the ones on the list, get the specific ages and let them know we'll set up the book club so that each day of the week corresponds with a different age bracket. I think that'd be more enjoyable for the kids because that'd put them with their friends from school and most likely with those on the same reading level."

"Except for kids like Kaden, who need a challenge," David said, obviously remembering Mandy's comment.

Laura laughed. She'd been around Mandy and her family a good bit this week because they were often in the gallery when she went to her apartment at night. Kaden was an adorable little boy, but he was one of the most inquisitive children she'd ever met. Laura now understood what his teacher meant by saying he needed a challenge. "I think Kaden could probably go with an older group of kids, as far as the reading level, but since they will be reading the books on their own and mainly talking about what they've read here, I think he'll enjoy being with his own age, don't you?"

"Yeah, I do," David agreed. He looked at Laura, and his attention moved to her cheek, where that wayward lock of hair curled against her skin. Laura knew what he was about to do, so she could have quickly tucked the strands out of the way herself, but for some strange reason, she didn't. Instead she held her breath as David tenderly slid his finger against her skin and eased the lock in place. "You're going to be an excellent teacher."

A tingle of *something* echoed from the point

where his finger touched her skin, ricocheting through her senses and then settling in her chest. Laura didn't know if the effect was from his compassionate touch or his earnest words. Or both.

Ready to get control of her emotions, she walked back to the children's area and said, "Zeb came by while you were gone. Come see what he did for us." She picked up the sketch pad from the table and turned it so David could see the drawing. "I'm going to make a boxcar to decorate the children's reading nook. If we use this design, they could climb inside and pretend they're on the actual boxcar while we talk about the story. We can use some of the beanbags and pillows already in the reading nook."

Even before she looked to verify the fact, she knew that David had moved closer to look at the drawing. She could sense the warmth of his body next to hers, and she turned to see that his face—as she suspected—was mere inches from her own. A hint of cologne teased the air, and she fought the urge to inhale…or move closer.

"It sounds like a great idea," he said. "Um, did Zeb mention how much he thought the materials would run?"

He couldn't disguise the worry in his tone, and it reinforced Laura's quest to make, rather than lose, money for his store. It also pulled her out of the uncomfortable moment of attraction that she was pretty sure only occurred on her side of this fence.

"He said since Diane Marsh's grandson is one of the kids participating in the book club, she'd probably donate the craft board and other materials we might need. And he said he thought you could make the wooden stands to hold the boxcar from crates that are usually kept behind the store."

The worry lines that'd shown on David's forehead as he'd looked at the drawing disappeared as his face slid into a grin. "Leave it to Zeb to get it all worked out. Zeb and you, I mean. This *is* a great idea, and if Diane will donate the materials, that'd make it even better."

"I'll go see her right now," Laura said. "I'd like to have it ready for First Friday."

David looked at the circular clock above the entrance showing straight-up noon. "You realize that's only six hours from now, right?"

"Then I'd better get busy." Laughing, she grabbed her purse and turned to leave, but then stopped when her cell started ringing the song "Daddy's Hands." "Hang on, that's my dad." Her father taught middle school history, and even though he was probably on his lunch break, she knew he never made personal calls from the school. She answered. "Daddy? Anything wrong?"

He exhaled thickly over the line. "Laura, I hate to bother you, and I sure don't want to worry you, but I need to ask…have you heard from your mother today?"

Laura had called her parents each night this week to let them know how things were going at the bookstore, how she was settling in, and then yesterday how the appointment with the new doctor had gone. But she hadn't heard from her mother since she hung up the phone with them last night. "I haven't. Did she leave again?"

"I don't know what's going on, hon, but it's been so much worse this year, since this summer. She isn't happy, and I honestly don't know what to do anymore. She wanted to go on that cruise in August, before I had to start back at the school, and I took her, but that still didn't help. And she wanted to go on regular dates, and we've been doing that, or trying to—she's been working more hours at the mall, you know." He sounded miserable, the way he always sounded whenever her mother did another round of leaving to "find herself."

"She isn't answering her cell?"

"Goes straight to voice mail. She must have it turned off."

"Was she supposed to work today?" Laura asked.

"She was, but Nan, the store manager, called me to see where she was this morning when she didn't show up at the store. I was afraid she'd had an accident or something, since she's never late for work, and I started trying to call her cell. And like I said, it went straight to voice mail. But I just called Nan back to see if she ever heard from her, and she said that your mother called in and said she was taking a personal day." He paused. "She'd assumed your mother would've called and told me."

"Of course she did," Laura said. Because that's what a normal wife would do. But something *was* different this time, because regardless of how many times Marjorie Holland had left without warning, she always planned her disappearances on her days off. She could leave Laura's father and Laura without any explanation whatsoever, but she would never miss a day of work and risk someone else taking her sales.

"I'll try calling her, but I'm sure you're right," Laura said. "If she doesn't want to talk to us, she won't."

"I know, dear. But, well, if you hear from her, will you call me, text me, whatever is more convenient? I just want to know that she's okay."

"I will, Daddy." She disconnected then immediately dialed her mother. Sure enough, it went straight to voice mail.

"She left again?" David asked.

Laura dropped the cell in her purse. "I don't know how he does it, goes through this over and over without any rhyme or reason to why she acts the way she does." For years, especially when she was younger, Laura would cry whenever her mother mysteriously disappeared. But those tears were done. Crying never helped, and Laura wasn't going to let her mother upset her now. It wasn't good for the babies if Laura was stressed, so she would *not* get stressed.

"You want to talk about it?" David asked, the concern in his voice evident.

She'd talked to David about her mother's peculiar behavior a few times when they were at UT, but she didn't want to spend their time today analyzing the mystery that was Marjorie Holland. "Nope. I want to go buy what we need to build a boxcar. Or rather, have it all donated to the cause."

He spotted a book out of order on a shelf, withdrew it and then began running his finger along the spines to find the correct spot. "Okay," he said, "but get some lunch while you're out. I don't want you forgetting to eat because you're trying to finish that boxcar."

"Don't worry." She pointed to her stomach. "They don't let me forget."

"That's good." He tapped a book as he apparently located where the misfiled one belonged, and then slid it into place. Then he leaned against the shelves and smiled. "And take your time. It shouldn't take all that long to make that prop, and I don't want you rushing to eat."

Laura liked his smile. "I won't rush," she promised.

Opening the door, she stepped outside, inhaled the crisp November air, took two steps down the sidewalk…and nearly ran smack-dab into her mom.

In a royal-blue pantsuit, gold jewelry and heels, Marjorie Holland looked as beautiful as ever. A peach Coach bag was draped over one shoulder. With her sleek blond hair and flawless complexion, she could easily pass for an older sister instead of Laura's mother. Then again, she was only seventeen years older and on top of that looked quite young for forty.

Her smile faltered a bit; she obviously was still preparing what she'd say when she found her daughter.

Laura waited and braced for the explanation.

She got none. Instead, Marjorie pulled out the beauty pageant smile, grabbed her in a hug and said, "Surprise!"

Chapter Five

Marjorie released Laura from the too-tight hug, leaned back and peered at her daughter. "Honey, pregnancy agrees with you. I believe you look even prettier."

"Thanks, Mom. But why didn't you tell me you were coming? Is everything okay?"

"Why, of course. I know you said that you were doing fine, but I just wanted to see for myself." She fingered the sleeve of Laura's dark green top. "Don't you love that blouse? I just knew it'd look adorable on you when I found it at the store. I got a great deal, you know."

"Thanks." Laura's mother had worked at Macy's, aka *the store*, for twenty years. She'd been the top salesperson in women's fashion for almost that long and lived for "great deals." The problem was, even with her employee discount, her addiction to sales typically ate up her paycheck. And Laura's father rarely said anything because she was always on the verge of leaving anyway without him giving her a reason to go. He'd often say that he was a timid personality and that Marjorie's fiery one was his perfect complement. Laura wasn't so sure.

"I brought you some more maternity clothes, also very stylish, for the last couple of months. You're going to *love* them," her mother said excitedly.

Laura already had so many clothes from Marjorie's previous purchases that she wasn't certain she'd be able to wear them all before the pregnancy was over. "Mom, I really have plenty already."

"Nonsense. You can never have too many clothes, or shoes." She held up her right leg for Laura to see her high-heeled boots. "How do you like these? The hue is called winter-peach. It's the latest complimentary color for the season. Fashion week paired it with everything. Aren't they amazing?"

"They're nice," Laura said, then shivered. She hadn't grabbed her cardigan because she'd planned to simply walk across the square to Scraps and Crafts. Little did she know she'd run into her mom and begin a lengthy chat session before she'd even crossed the sidewalk.

"Oh, my, why aren't you wearing that cute gold cardigan I bought you? You don't need to get chilled," her mother said.

"I have it in the store, but it's really not that cold, as long as you don't stay outside overly long." Laura pointed to the craft store. "I was going to Scraps and

Crafts to get some things for a project I want to do today and also get some lunch."

"Well, why don't we do lunch first and then I'll help you get the craft items you need?"

"That sounds great." Despite her mother's quirks, Laura did enjoy spending time with her when she was in one of her happy moods, and she appeared to be in one today, in spite of—or maybe because of—the fact that she'd left Nashville without any word to her husband.

"Wonderful. I can drive. Where would you like to go? What's near here?" She dug around in her purse then withdrew her keys.

Laura smiled. "This—" she waved her hand toward the shops that composed the town square "—*is* what's around here."

Marjorie's blue eyes widened, and she plunked her keys back in her bag. "Well, okay, then." She scanned the storefronts. "So…where do we eat?"

"Come on, I'll show you." Laura led the way to Nelson's Variety Store, her mother's boots clicking the sidewalk with every step.

Marjorie stopped when they reached the tiny black-and-white tiles that formed the entrance to the five-and-dime. "Here?"

Laura opened the door. "Come on, it's really good."

Her mother visibly swallowed, her smile slipping again, but then she quickly recovered and headed in as though she owned the place.

"Well, hello, Miss Laura," Marvin Tolleson said as they entered. "Who's your friend?" He guided them to a red vinyl booth near the old-fashioned soda fountain.

"Mr. Marvin, this is my mother, Marjorie Holland. Mom, this is Marvin Tolleson. He and his wife, Mae, own the variety store, and they serve the best cheeseburger and sweet potato fries you'll ever taste." Laura and David had shared lunch here twice this week already, and she'd loved every bite.

"Cheeseburgers," Marjorie said, again fighting to hold her smile in place. "Why that sounds... delicious."

Laura couldn't remember ever seeing her mother eat a cheeseburger. In fact, the majority of the time she dined on a salad with grilled chicken and fat-free dressing. "They have salads, too," she said. "But the burgers are the best."

"We do have salads," Marvin agreed. "But they don't stick to your ribs like a good ol' burger. All Angus beef, too."

"You don't say." Marjorie lifted the laminated single page of the menu and flipped it, looking for the rest of the available items. There weren't any, so she slowly turned the page back over.

"Why don't I get your drinks while you're deciding," Marvin offered, unfazed by her mother's lack of enthusiasm.

"Water with lemon please," she said.

"Okay, and you want your extra large lemonade, Miss Laura?"

"You know I do." She'd grown very fond of Mr. Marvin, and of all the Claremont residents she'd met so far. They weren't pretentious, nothing showy or ostentatious. In fact, she'd say they were as down-to-earth as anyone she'd ever known. Her family wasn't rich, but you'd never know that by the way her mother dressed and carried herself. Her father, on the other hand, was proud of his teaching job and never put on a show. He was most comfortable in a pullover and jeans or khakis, and he didn't try to talk or act like he was something he wasn't.

"I'm going to the restroom, dear. If he comes back for the order, just get me a salad with the fat-free dressing, okay?"

Laura had hoped her mother *might* forego her routine for their day together, but she should've known better. "I will."

Marjorie clicked across the floor to the bathrooms with every head in the restaurant watching her move, and Laura waited for her to disappear before pulling her cell phone from her purse. She quickly sent a text to her father.

She's here. She's fine. I'll let you know when she starts back home. And I'll let you know if I figure out what's going on.

Marvin returned with the drinks and Laura ordered their food. Then her phone buzzed with a text from her father. Undoubtedly he was teaching a class, but he must have had his cell on hand in case he heard anything from his runaway wife.

I'm so glad she's okay. Please keep me posted. Love you.

Laura sent a quick text—I love you, too, Daddy—and dropped the phone back in her purse at the exact moment her mother exited the restroom. She felt so sorry for her dad, never being able to figure out the woman he loved so much. And part of her felt sorry for her mother, too, attempting to appear happy and content when obviously she was anything but.

Marjorie gracefully slid into the booth. She didn't do anything that looked unrehearsed, and even the way she sat appeared camera-ready. She'd won Miss Teen for Davidson County when she was merely sixteen, an accomplishment heralded in countless photos around their home. In Laura's opinion, her mother still acted as though she were being scored for poise on a daily basis. "Did you order?" she asked, unfolding the paper napkin and placing it on her lap.

"I did."

They sat for a moment in an awkward silence, Laura not knowing what to say and her mother smiling politely at each person who passed the booth but not speaking to anyone. She had a regal air about her, and she definitely stood out amid the others gathering for lunch in the five-and-dime. Most folks sitting in booths or at the soda fountain had on long-sleeved T-shirts or sweaters with a pair of jeans and sneakers. A few wore khakis, and one lady had on a plaid dress, but hardly any jobs on the square required a strict dress code. At Macy's, Marjorie dressed like she was ready for a photo shoot each day and was the most requested salesperson for help with style. However, even today, when she knew she wasn't going to work, she dressed the same way. She didn't have any dress-down clothes and probably wouldn't wear them even if she did.

The silence continued, until her mother obviously couldn't take it anymore. "I had to get away," she whispered. Then, as if in afterthought, she added, "And I did want to see how you were doing."

"Why did you have to get away?" Laura asked quietly. The booths and tables were all very close together so that customers could easily converse with those around them. When she and David had eaten here before, they'd almost always chatted with people at the other tables nearby. But there'd be no way anyone else could jump in on this conversation. Laura didn't even know what was going on with her mom; how would anyone else?

As if she also suspected someone was listening,

Marjorie lowered her voice again. "I just did, you know. It's…hard to explain."

Obviously. She'd been doing it as long as Laura could remember, and no one had received an explanation yet.

Marjorie lifted her fork, inspected it as though looking for smudges, then returned it to the table. "So…how *are* you doing?"

"I'm fine," Laura said, choosing not to dwell on the subject her mother refused to talk about; it wouldn't help anyway. "I love it here, and I think the job at the bookstore is going to be perfect until I'm able to get hired in the school system."

A man at the booth behind her mother turned and leaned around the edge. "Sorry, but I couldn't help overhearing, and I thought you'd like to know that Mrs. Jackson, the kindergarten teacher, is retiring at the end of this year. You might want to go ahead and put your resumé in at the elementary school. Or if you're looking for something at the middle school, Mr. Nance, the eighth grade teacher, is leaving after this semester, so they'll need someone for his spot in January."

Laura felt her heartbeat increase at her excitement. There was no way she could take a teaching job in January, since she'd have just had the babies, but a kindergarten position starting next school year? That'd be perfect! "Thanks for letting me know…." She knew she'd seen him before but couldn't remember the name.

"Aidan," he said. "Aidan Lee. And you're working with David at the bookstore, aren't you? I came by earlier this week to bring him the information for my sister-in-law's book signing next Saturday."

"Yes, I am," she said. "And I remember meeting you now. Aidan, this is my mother, Marjorie Holland."

He extended a hand. "Really? You're her mom. I'd have guessed sister."

Laura watched her mother beam.

"Aw, thank you," she said, her hand fluttering in front of her face the way it always did when she faked embarrassment. Laura knew she loved this, but Laura didn't mind; her mother was beautiful, and it was nice to see her look sincerely happy, even if it took a bout of flattery to make it happen.

"Well, I'll let y'all get back to your visit, and I'll try not to eavesdrop—" he grinned "—too much."

Laura and her mother laughed.

"Is everyone here that friendly?" Marjorie attempted to whisper, but Laura thought Aidan probably heard. Even so, he remained facing the other direction.

"They are. Just wait until you meet the people I'm renting my apartment from. They've been so nice."

"Maybe when we get done with lunch you can show it to me. I saw the Carter Photography building," Marjorie said. "That's the one you said you're staying at, right?"

"Yes, the apartment is above her gallery. I was thrilled that Mandy and Daniel offered it for rent. And they're only charging me two hundred a month."

"Seriously? How can they afford to rent it for so cheap?"

"I'm pretty sure they aren't doing it for extra money, but they knew I wouldn't accept it for free."

"Amazing," her mother said as Marvin returned with a huge salad topped with bacon, boiled eggs and grilled chicken and placed the bowl in front of her. Then he gave Laura her plate, covered completely with a big juicy cheeseburger and a small mountain of sweet potato fries.

"That's..." Marjorie eased the bowl away a little, as though she couldn't take it all in while it was so close. "That's the biggest salad I've ever seen."

"Biggest one we make," Marvin said with a grin. Then he looked a little confused. "That is the one you ordered, isn't it, Miss Laura?"

Laura laughed. "Yes, it is."

"So y'all have everything you need?" he asked.

"We do," she said and waited for her mother's complaint. Marjorie didn't disappoint.

"Did you really think I could eat all of this?" she asked.

"I knew you'd never order the monster salad, but

I also knew it wouldn't hurt you to splurge every now and then." To her relief, her mother's face split into a smile.

"I am hungry," she admitted.

Laura suspected her mother was often hungry, but she wouldn't say that now. Instead, she'd enjoy seeing her mother eat enough to fill her up for a change.

They chatted throughout the meal, with Laura carefully staying away from the subject of why Marjorie had really left Nashville this time, and when they were done, Laura was pleasantly surprised to see her mother had eaten every bite of her salad *and* a few of Laura's sweet potato fries.

"Oh, my, I'm absolutely stuffed," she said.

Laura nodded in agreement. "Same here, but it's a good stuffed, and I'm pretty sure the twins are content. They aren't moving."

"You were that way," Marjorie said, "always quiet and still after I ate. And then, of course, you'd try to dance your way through the night."

Laura dabbed her napkin at her mouth and then tossed it on her empty plate. "They wake me up every now and then, too."

Marjorie picked up the check, glanced at the amount and then placed the cash on the table. "I've got this."

Laura knew better than to argue. "Thanks, Mom."

They started to leave, but Aidan climbed out of

his booth. "Hey, before you go, I wanted to tell you something about Destiny's book signing."

"Okay." So far Laura had learned that Destiny had recently married Aidan's brother, Troy, and had her first book coming out this month. The book was a collection of love stories based in Claremont, and she had a contract to write several more love-story books for cities all across the South. Laura looked forward to meeting the new author and also to figuring out how she could best promote Destiny…and garner some sales for David's bookstore.

"I forgot to tell y'all the other day that she's got a Facebook page, and she's already got a few thousand fans just from the publicity her publisher has done and word of mouth."

"A few *thousand?* That's terrific." Laura sensed that next Saturday's book signing had the potential to be much bigger than the "small friends and family" gathering that David had said he anticipated for the event.

"Yeah, we're all pretty excited for her," Aidan said, "but the part I wanted to tell you about is that we set up an event for her book signing at A Likely Story. I haven't checked it today, but yesterday she already had two hundred people that said they were coming. Just wanted to make sure David ordered enough books."

Laura couldn't believe it. David hadn't ordered nearly that many books. This would be wonderful for business next week and also great exposure for the bookstore with all of those people coming in. Laura would definitely want to have book club information available for adults. Maybe she'd see about having the adult book club start out with Destiny's book, and Destiny could be a guest author for one of their meetings. "That's great news, Aidan! David's got a Facebook page for the bookstore, too. He hasn't done a lot with it, but we were talking about updating and promoting it better. He wanted me to work on it, and I'll get started right away."

"Cool," he said, then nodded to Marjorie. "Nice to meet you, Mrs. Holland."

"You, too." She waited until they were out of the store, then said, "That was a nice-looking young man, don't you think?"

"I'm not looking, Mom."

"As I recall, David is a nice-looking man also. Very nice-looking, I'd say. And he's been a real friend, hasn't he? Sounds like his bookstore is doing well, too."

Laura wasn't going to comment on David's attractiveness, particularly since she'd only recently noticed just how appealing her friend was…and because she didn't want her mother to think there was any chance of a relationship between them. They were friends, and that was that.

She walked beside her mom toward the craft store and wondered whether she should address the other point of her mother's statement—David's business. She could voice her concerns for the financial state of the place, but she wouldn't. Laura needed her parents to feel good about her move here, and she also believed that David's store would become profitable, eventually. The book club was gaining kids by the day, and it appeared the book signing he'd lined up for Destiny Lee was going to bring in plenty of customers, too. Yes, with Laura's help, it would be just fine.

"I really enjoy working there. And I honestly believe the experience will help me be a better teacher. We're starting a children's book club. That's why I need the items from the craft store, to make a prop for their story area."

"I'm just glad you're happy," her mother said, and Laura could tell she meant every word. "David, well, he cares about you, Laura. A guy who'd help you the way he has this week, *that's* the kind you need to look for."

"I told you," Laura said, forcing a smile as she opened the door to Scraps and Crafts, "I'm not looking."

"I know, dear, but when you do, I want to make sure you find someone who cares about you. You want a man who chooses *you*."

The last few words didn't make sense to Laura. A man who chooses her? As opposed to...what? But before she could ask, an older woman standing amid the quilting supplies hurriedly crossed the store to meet them.

"Welcome to Scraps and Crafts," she said. "I'm Diane Marsh." She noticed Laura's tummy leading the way and smiled. "I'm guessing you're Laura Holland."

"I'm not the only pregnant woman in town, am I?"

"No, Hannah Graham is expecting, too, but you're the only one that I knew was pregnant and would be coming over to get supplies to make a boxcar."

"How did you know that?"

"Zeb. He called and asked if I could get the materials together for you because he was afraid you'd try to carry them to the bookstore yourself. He said you didn't need to be toting that kind of weight in your condition."

Laura grinned. "He never stops helping people, does he?"

"No, he doesn't. He also said that you're the one organizing that book club I signed my grandson Andy up for, and he asked if I'd be willing to donate the materials for your prop."

"Did he leave anything for me to do?" Laura asked.

"Yes, he said he wanted you to meet me!" Diane laughed, and Laura and Marjorie joined in.

"Well, it's nice to meet you," Laura said. "And this is my mother, Marjorie Holland."

"Pleasure to meet you," Marjorie said, shaking Diane's hand.

"You, too," Diane answered.

Laura could tell the lady was surprised at the fact that her mother was young. She'd seen that same look anytime she introduced her mother growing up, and she suspected that would never change. "I'll probably make my way over to the bookstore tonight during First Friday so I can see the boxcar once it's finished."

"Do you think I can get it done today?" Laura glanced at her watch. "It's twelve forty-five."

"Sure you can," Diane said, "especially since you'll have help."

"Help?"

"Hannah Graham, the woman I mentioned that is also expecting. She was in here shopping for supplies to decorate her nursery when Zeb called. I told her about the book club, but she'd already heard about it from Mandy and signed up her little Autumn. Anyway, Hannah's a stay-at-home mom now, but before that she would design all of the store windows in the square. She's very talented with props, and when I told her about the boxcar, she said she'd like to help. More than likely, she's already working on it." Diane smiled. "I saw her head to the bookstore when she left here."

"She carried the materials over?" Laura asked,

wishing she and her mother had come to the craft store first.

"Oh, no, David picked those up for you. He was evidently on the same page as Zeb and didn't want you toting them."

"Everybody's watching out for me around here, aren't they?" Laura asked.

"That's what folks 'round here do," Diane said. "It makes us feel useful."

"Well, I should go help Hannah."

"Nah, you visit with your mom. Hannah is used to creating on her own, and she said she had a lot of energy to use up. She's only in her first trimester, but she's already nesting. I'm sure you haven't had a chance to decorate your nursery yet, since you just got to town. Let me know when you get ready, and I'll help you out. Hannah will, too, I'm sure, if you'd like additional input."

Laura didn't even know whether she had a nursery to decorate, but she nodded. "I'll let you know."

They left the craft shop and immediately saw that several vendors were already setting up booths along the sidewalks and in the center of the square.

"Wow, what's going on?" her mother asked.

"Tonight is the First Friday event. David said they have it every month, and it's a chance for all of the local artists and entertainers to perform, as well as the merchants to showcase their items. That's why we're trying to get the boxcar prop done by tonight."

Laura stopped to look at some colorful wooden puzzles an elderly man had already placed out for viewing. He sat behind the table steadily carving pieces. A woman with a silver bun and a patchwork dress sat beside him painting a completed ballerina puzzle. The pieces stood up from the stand, so little hands would easily be able to drop them in place. "That's so pretty."

The woman pulled her paintbrush across the edge of the ballerina's skirt and looked up at Laura. "Thank you, dear. We can put your baby's name on one if you'd like." She smiled. "You having a boy or a girl?"

"Two girls," Marjorie answered before Laura had a chance.

"Twins!" She put her paintbrush down and placed her palms together as though she were praying. "Well, that's a real Christmas present, isn't it?"

Laura nodded. "Yes, it is." She ran a finger along one of the ballerina puzzles that had already dried. "I still haven't picked the girls' names yet, but when I do, I'd like to get them these puzzles. They won't be able to put them together for a while, but when they can, I'd really like them to have these."

"Do you have a business card?" Marjorie asked.

"We sure do," the man said. He'd finished carving and pulled a small card from his shirt pocket. Handing it to Laura, he said, "I will pray for an easy delivery and two beautiful healthy babies. That's quite a blessing you've got there, young lady."

Laura smiled. "Thank you, and I know."

She and her mother continued across the square, all of the booths tempting them with every step.

"Look at those wreaths," her mother said. "I haven't seen anything like them. Are they made of ribbon, or is that something else?" She pointed to the red, green and gold Christmas wreaths that seemed to change color in the sunlight.

"I'm not sure." Laura realized she would love to browse all of the booths with her mother, but she needed to get back to the bookstore and build the boxcar. "Mom, why don't you spend the night tonight? We could see all of the First Friday booths, and then tomorrow the town is adding even more for the Holiday Crafters Extravaganza, with everything geared around Thanksgiving and Christmas." She knew she'd have to call and explain to her dad, but she also knew that he'd want her to spend some quality time with her mom, if Marjorie were willing to stay.

Which she wasn't.

"Oh, honey, I was going to tell you that I probably need to head on home after we get you back to the bookstore. I have to work in the morning, you know. I had thought I'd have a chance to take a peek at your apartment, but I don't think it's going to work this time."

"Right. I wasn't thinking."

"But I need to go get that bag of clothes for you out of the car. I'm parked behind the toy store. Why don't you head on back to the bookstore, and I'll grab it and bring it to you before I go. That way I can see David before I leave."

Laura didn't know why she thought her mother might actually want to spend more than a little time with her. "Sure, that'd be fine."

Marjorie clicked her way toward Tiny Tots Treasure Box and then disappeared down the sidewalk leading to the parking area, while Laura, feeling defeated, went back to A Likely Story. Entering, she was surprised that the first thing she saw was the top of what appeared to be a red boxcar peeking above the bookshelves in the back right corner of the store. "Oh, my!"

"Whoops, we're caught. She's back," David said.

Laura heard a child's laugh, then some scuffling as someone apparently tripped, and then he stepped around the nearest endcap grinning and looking guilty.

"You've already finished it?" Laura asked.

"Not all of it," he said. "We were trying to get it done and surprise you, but you got back quicker than we thought. I figured you'd spend a little more time with your mom."

"You knew Mom was coming?" she asked, shocked.

He shook his head. "No, but Aidan Lee came by

to see if I'd gotten in that graphics book he needed for school, and he mentioned that he'd met your mother at Nelson's."

"Did he tell you about Destiny Lee's event page for the signing?" she asked.

"He did, and I ordered more books. I have to admit, it surprised me, but in a good way."

She liked the way his eyes held a glint of excitement when he told her about ordering those books. She wanted to give him lots of reasons to look like that, and she hoped to start tonight when she signed up a bunch of kids for the book club. "And so you decided you'd surprise *me* in a good way by building the boxcar on your own?"

"Nope, we're helping!"

Laura recognized Kaden's voice, and then he peeked from behind a book stack to verify the fact. "You're helping?" she asked.

He nodded. "Yep." He motioned for Laura to follow him, and she did. "See, me and Autumn are helping my mom and Miss Hannah. Miss Hannah is the best at drawing and painting and stuff, but Autumn and I have been really good at making the nail marks, haven't we, Miss Hannah?"

A woman with short brown hair and a streak of brown paint on her cheek stood up from where she and Mandy had been painting the lower half of a ladder extending down the right side of the boxcar.

"Hey, I'm Hannah Graham. I hope you don't mind

us working on your reading prop. I used to be a window designer for the square before I married Matt, and this project reminded me of how much fun it is."

"I don't mind at all."

"And I'm Autumn." A beautiful little girl sat beside the boxcar with a black marker in hand.

"Nice to meet you, Autumn, and thank you for helping with the boxcar," Laura said.

"You're welcome," she said, then turned her attention back to the nail marks she'd been making with the marker.

"Hey, Laura," Mandy said with a wave of a paint-splattered hand.

"Hi, Mandy. Thanks for helping."

"Kaden hasn't stopped talking about the book club. When he found out there was the possibility of a boxcar they could climb in, he wanted to make certain that happened. And the kids only had a half day of school today, so this gave us something to do."

"That's right," Kaden said, pumping a fist in the air. "Fall break starts today!"

"Fall break for Claremont coincides with the Holiday Crafters Extravaganza," Hannah explained.

Laura noticed Hannah and Autumn wore matching pink overalls. Hannah's had a stretchy pouch for a potentially expanding stomach, but her pregnancy was barely showing. "Diane told me you're

tension in the room and giving Laura the impressio
that she'd literally been saved by the bell.

"I guess Mandy forgot that she'd wanted som
tea. I'll go take care of the kettle," David said, turn
ing and heading to the back of the store and leavin
Laura alone to deal with her mother.

"Anything you want to tell me?" Marjorie aske

"No." Laura wondered if short and to-the-poi
would work.

It didn't. Her mother forged ahead with the inte
rogation. "Didn't you see the way he looked at you
And in case you're wondering what you look lik
when you look at him, it's pretty much the sam
thing."

"I'm emotional now," Laura said. "That's all. An
he's protective, like any good friend would be for
friend that's pregnant."

A buzz sounded from her mother's purse, an
Marjorie placed the bag of clothes on the neares
table and then fished out her cell. She glanced at th
display. "That was Thomas. He's called eight time
today, left five messages."

Laura wished she'd texted her father and give
him another update, but she hadn't had time sinc
lunch. He was probably finishing his school day no
and wondering if he'd have a wife at home tonigh
"Why didn't you tell Daddy you were coming here?
Laura figured it didn't hurt to ask what she reall

also expecting," Laura said, "but I think I've got you beat in the baby bump department."

Hannah laughed. "Check back with me in seven months."

"In seven months, I'm hoping we'll swap looks. You can go for this—" she pointed to her tummy "—and I'll be happy with that."

They all laughed, with David's masculine rumble standing out from the rest. Laura quieted her own laughter so she could listen to the beauty of his. He seemed to notice where her attention had landed because his eyes caught hers, and she felt her cheeks blush before she turned her attention to the others. Then, as the chuckles died down, Laura heard the bell on the door and then the telltale clicking of her mother's heels working their way through the store.

"Laura?" she called. She found them all in the children's area and gave her best smile. "Well, hello." She held up an oversize Macy's bag dangling from her right arm. "Got your clothes."

"Wow, that's a bunch of clothes," Kaden said.

Laura explained, "She buys me too much, I think," and then before she hurt her mom's feelings, she added, "but I do appreciate them, Mom. Thanks."

"You're welcome," Marjorie said. Then Laura began the introductions.

"Everyone, this is my mom, Marjorie Holland. Mom, this is Hannah, Mandy, Kaden and Autumn. And you already know David."

Her mother said a brief hello to the others and then turned her entire attention on David. "It's so good to see you again," she said. "And it—well, it means so much to us that you're helping Laura get settled here. We'd have loved for her to stay in Nashville, you know, but she wanted a fresh start. And I have to admit, from everything I've seen so far of Claremont, this is a wonderful place to have a family."

David looked from Marjorie to Laura. "I was very happy that she knew she could come here."

Laura swallowed. His words said so much. She hadn't been certain that she'd made the right choice when she'd arrived in Claremont. She hadn't *known* that she could come here. She'd *hoped*, but she hadn't known. However, throughout the week, with every passing day, she learned and believed without a doubt that she had come to the right place. "Thank you, David."

"Okay, I think we're done," Hannah said, snapping the lid on a small paint can.

"But I can put lots more nail marks," Kaden said.

"I know you can," Mandy responded, "but it's got just the right amount now, so we don't want to overdo it. And we need to get ready for First Friday. You promised to help me at the shop, remember?"

"Oh, yeah, right." Kaden grabbed up his markers and handed them to Hannah. "Thanks for teaching me how to make nail marks, Miss Hannah."

"You're welcome," she said.

Autumn followed suit, handing her markers to her mother. Hannah put all of the markers and paints in a big green tote, hoisted it on her arm and then took Autumn's hand. "Okay, we'll see all of you at First Friday." She took another look at the boxcar. "Turned out great. Tell Zeb he did a super job on the design."

"I will," Laura said.

Marjorie said goodbye to each of them and promised she'd see them again on her next visit to Claremont. Then David walked them all to the door while Marjorie and Laura marveled at the incredible reading area. "It looks terrific, Laura. And it was so nice of your new friends to do all of this for you."

"I know." She was overwhelmed with gratitude. An hour ago, she hadn't been certain the boxcar would have been done by the time First Friday started. But now, it wasn't even 2:00 p.m. and it was finished. "This is amazing."

"That's what I think, too," David said, returning to stand beside them.

Laura turned to see his reaction to the completed boxcar, but he wasn't looking at the prop. Instead, he was focused intently…on her. And Laura was pretty sure she wasn't the only one who noticed. Her mother's perfectly arched brows lifted and her blue eyes studied Laura's friend-slash-boss.

A whistle sounded from the kitchen, breaking the

wanted to know. If her mother got mad, she was about to leave anyway.

But rather than telling Laura she should mind her own business, Marjorie merely turned and walked toward the front of the store. Laura followed, thinking that she was going to walk out without answering the question. But her mother stopped, peered toward the back and apparently realized that David was still occupied in the kitchen…and the two of them were completely alone.

"I'm sorry," Laura said, uncertain whether she meant the apology or not, but this was the way it went. Her mother got mad or got her feelings hurt, and Laura—or, more typically, her father—apologized.

"This year has been tougher than all the others," Marjorie whispered, staring out the window at the crafters setting up their booths.

"Why?" Laura asked.

Her head shook slightly, but she didn't answer her daughter's question. Instead, she continued, "Did I ever tell you your daddy took me to the fair? It was on our first date. He spent every dollar in his pocket trying to win me this big white teddy bear, and on the last throw, he did." She smiled, and a single tear flitted its way across her cheekbone. She didn't wipe it away, and it traced a slow path toward her neck, while Laura watched in awe.

She'd seen her mother mad, seen her upset. But she'd *never* seen her cry. "Mom?"

"I'd say I fell in love with Thomas when he finally won that bear, but I'd loved him well before that. I think I loved him the first time I saw him, you know. On the playground in junior high. I'd just moved to Nashville and it was my first day at a new school, and I saw him, and it was…I just knew." Another sad smile. "I've loved him ever since, I suppose."

Laura had never been more confused. Her head pounded, and her mind raced for the right words. But nothing her mother said made sense. She'd kept her father on edge for years with her running away, coming back, being sad, being happy. She was like Forrest Gump's box of chocolates—you never knew what you were going to get.

"This year, with you, the pregnancy and Jared… It's just—been hard for me. I'm so sorry. I'm happy for you, and I want you happy. I want you to have… everything you want. I'd have loved for you to stay with us, but I understand. It would be hard to start a life where Jared is starting his new one. I wouldn't want to do it." Still looking away from Laura and toward the square, she shrugged one shoulder. "But I wouldn't know about starting on my own. I'm glad, though. I'm glad that you didn't end up with Jared. You deserve to be the one somebody chooses. If you aren't, then—" another shrug "—then you always wonder, don't you?"

"Mom? Are you talking about Daddy? Or…what?"

Marjorie turned, and both of her eyes were now swimming in tears, wet smudges of mascara marring her perfect makeup. "David. You may not see it yet, and you may not even want it yet, but that boy…he would choose you."

Laura's head was reeling, and she felt exactly the same way she did when she'd had the morning sickness so terribly. But this wasn't the babies making her queasy. It was her mother. "Mama, Daddy chose you. He married you, and he loves you. He told me so today."

She smiled again, but like before, it didn't reach her eyes. "I knew he'd call you. He's precious, isn't he?"

"Yes, he is," Laura said, and immediately recalled that she'd used the exact same word to describe David. "Why do you keep leaving him the way you do? He doesn't know, but he wants to. If you tell him what's wrong, I honestly believe he'll fix it."

She shook her head again. "He can't. And after all of the reminders of this year are done, I'll be better again. I feel sure of it."

"You're saying you don't think Daddy chose you when he married you? If he didn't then who did he choose?"

Marjorie turned, hugged Laura tightly again and kissed her cheek. "I'm going home now." Then, without another word, she walked out the door.

Shaken, Laura watched the blue pantsuit disappear in the crowd, her mother's head bowed and looking at the ground as she walked, her posture a direct opposite of her typical confident gait. What had just happened? Laura felt like she'd finally glimpsed a little of what her mother kept hidden so well, but she still didn't understand, not at all. And that realization sucker punched her. She grabbed a gasp of air, turned to release her cry…and sank into David's embrace.

"Shhh," he soothed, holding her close and running a hand up and down her spine. "I'm here. I'm right here."

Chapter Six

David had returned from the kitchen in time to hear the last of Marjorie's disjointed conversation, see her walk out the door and then witness Laura's reaction. Holding her in his arms seemed the natural thing to do, to provide comfort to his friend when she was hurting. Before this week, he'd never felt gratitude for his store being empty, but he did now. Because with the solitude came the ability to hold her as long as she needed. He ran his palm gently down her hair, while her face was still buried against his chest.

"It'll be okay," he said, and he prayed that it would. Laura had mentioned her mother's moodiness through college, but what David saw a moment ago was more than moodiness. Marjorie Holland was an emotional roller coaster. No wonder Laura didn't want to stay there to raise her little girls.

She shifted her head to the side, wiped her hand beneath her eyes and inhaled deeply. Then she wiggled out of his embrace and swiped under her eyes again. "Some employee I'm turning out to be, huh? Bursting into tears the first week on the job." One corner of her mouth lifted in a half smile. "Ready to fire me?"

David wished she'd have let him hold her a little longer. He could tell she was still upset, but he could also tell she was ready to move on. He'd let her. "Why would I fire the one person who's been able to bring paying customers? I've never had that much success at it. Just ask my accountant." He hadn't intended to say anything that would indicate his business wasn't going well, so he attempted a laugh and changed the subject. "Hey, I made that tea for Mandy. Might as well drink it. You want some?"

"Sure."

He started toward the back.

"And David?"

He stopped, turned. "Yeah?"

"Thanks. Not just for the tea, but for...everything."

"You're welcome." He prepared the tea and returned to find her sitting in front of the boxcar and talking on her phone.

"Yes, she left a few minutes ago. She should be there in about four hours. No, she didn't tell me," she said into the cell. Looking up, she mouthed "thanks" when he placed the tea on the table beside her.

Wanting to give her privacy, he went to the computer at the counter and checked on the number of people registered to attend Destiny Lee's signing. When he'd looked this afternoon, the number was just over 200. Now it was 283. "Wow."

"What is it?" Laura asked when she'd hung up, leaning over the counter to see the monitor.

"There are nearly three hundred people registered for Destiny's signing next Saturday. We'll need to set up the tent outside and have them line up on the sidewalk."

"That's awesome." She smiled and looked like she was feeling better, her eyes clearing up from her tears.

"You talked to your dad?"

She took a sip of her tea and nodded. "Yes. Mom said something about him not choosing her. I have no idea what she was talking about, but it didn't seem like something to ask him on the phone. But he said he's coming here the day after Thanksgiving. We can talk then."

"The day *after* Thanksgiving? Aren't your parents coming here for the holiday to see you? Or are you not going there?"

She took another sip of tea. "Our family has never done the typical Thanksgiving thing because Mom doesn't want to have to cook a big dinner and get exhausted on Thanksgiving and then work all day on Black Friday. And she refuses to take off on Black Friday because it's the biggest sale day of the year.

Macy's opens at midnight Thanksgiving night and stays open for twenty-three hours straight. It's a pretty big deal for Mom."

David thought Thanksgiving was a pretty big deal for most moms, but he wouldn't point that out. Instead, he asked, "So you'll be here for Thanksgiving?"

"Yeah, I don't want to drive all the way to Nashville and back when they aren't doing anything for the holiday. Our family dinner is just three people anyway—my grandparents have all passed on, and I'm an only child. Plus Dad is driving here on Black Friday since she'll be working all day. I told him I was sure we'd have a big sale at the bookstore, too, and he offered to help us out."

"You don't have to work that day," David said. "You can visit with him."

"I know I don't have to. I want to. We're liable to sell all sorts of books that people can give for Christmas presents. We'll want to stock up with the most popular ones, you know."

He grinned. He may not have known how he could pay her, but it appeared if all of her sales ideas were right, she might actually save his business. "Okay, but if you're staying here for Thanksgiving you're going to have a real dinner. My folks are coming in for the holiday."

"Oh, no, I am *not* going to intrude on your family dinner."

He shook his head. "You aren't. Mom isn't about to travel all the way from South Florida and then cook, and I'm pathetic in the kitchen."

She held up her cup. "Your tea is good."

"I can handle tea and eggs. And grilling. Any guy can grill, but that's it."

"So do y'all go out to eat on Thanksgiving?" she asked.

"Nah, we join the others in town who have dinner at the church. Everybody brings a dish, and we all share. It's fun, and we have some amazing cooks in Claremont. The best way to go for Thanksgiving. Trust me, you'll like it."

She looked skeptical. "But I'm not a church member there. And I haven't even visited."

"That isn't a prerequisite," he said, liking the idea of helping her have her first "real" Thanksgiving dinner. "It's for the community, and you're part of the Claremont community now."

"Yeah, I guess I am, aren't I?"

The bell on the front door sounded, and two dark-haired boys darted in, ran past David and Laura at the counter and made a beeline for the boxcar.

"Look, there it is!" one said.

"Yep, Kaden was right," the other answered, while Clint Hayes entered the bookstore smiling and shaking his head.

"Hey, David, I'm assuming Matthew and Daniel found their way to the boxcar?" he asked.

"They ran by so fast I can't for certain say it was the twins," David said.

"That pretty much guarantees it was them." He looked to Laura. "Clint Hayes. Please forgive my boys. I'd like to say this isn't normal, but that'd be lying. Their mother jokes that we spent a lot of their first year trying to work them up to walking and we've spent the next nine trying to get them to slow down."

Laura laughed. "They look adorable, from what I saw of them. David's right, though, they moved pretty fast."

The boys chatted away as they climbed in and around the boxcar, while their dad picked up a couple of *Boxcar Children* books from the stack by the register.

"They're excited about the book club," he said. "That's a great idea, David." He withdrew his wallet and gave David the money for the books.

"The idea was Laura's. She and I went to UT together, and she's helping me out at the bookstore until she begins teaching. She's hoping to get a job at Claremont Elementary after she has her babies."

"Babies? You're having twins?"

"I am," Laura said.

"Twins are cool!" one of the boys called from the reading nook.

"Twin boys?" the other one yelled.

Laura laughed. "Actually, twin girls."

One of the kids emitted an "Eww," and Clint quickly responded. "Matthew, that's enough."

"Well, at least it's twins, even if it's girls," the other one added.

Laura laughed again, and David liked hearing it, especially after she'd been so upset by her mother's unusual departure.

"Twins are a lot of fun, even if they can be a hand-ful," Clint said, taking his change from David. "By the way, the boys said all of the kids in their class at school were going to join your boxcar club. I think the majority of them are coming in tonight. That's why we came early. My wife thought it'd be smart to beat the rush."

"That's a good idea," Laura said. "And because we do expect a lot of kids to sign up, we're going to offer the book club each weekday after school. It'll start at three-thirty and last an hour." She reached past David to a stack of clipboards with signup sheets. David hadn't realized she'd already prepared the sheets, but she had each one labeled and ready to go. He'd been impressed with her organizational skills throughout the week and now she'd impressed him again.

"You really are going to be an amazing teacher," he said, as she handed Clint a pen to sign up the twins.

Clint put both of the kids on the Monday sheet. "We'll go with Monday, since that one says it's for nine-and ten-year-olds. The boys are ten. Plus Nathan and Autumn are down for that day. They're in the boys' class at school."

"Sounds good," Laura said.

"Cool! We're with Nathan and Autumn," Matthew told Daniel, still playing inside the boxcar.

"Awesome!" Daniel yelled.

"Okay, boys, we've got to go pick up your mom at the school. Let's go. You can come back here tonight and play in the boxcar during First Friday."

"Awwww," one of the boys grumbled.

"It won't be long," Clint stressed. Then he said to Laura, "My wife teaches fourth grade. I'll let her know you're looking for a job and have her stop by to meet you tonight. She can tell you what you need to do to apply when you're ready. And congratulations again on your twins. They really are a lot of fun."

"Thanks," Laura said as the boys ran by in a flash.

"Bye!" they yelled, brushing past their father as they flew out the door. "Last one to the fountain is a rotten egg!"

"And here we go. Pray for all of the vendors, and that my kids won't take out too many booths," Clint said, heading out the door.

"That's two different people who've tried to help me today with finding a job at the school," she said.

"Nothing unusual about that. People help each other out. That's what we're supposed to do." David grabbed two *Boxcar Children* books from the case behind the counter and replaced the two he'd just sold Clint on the display stacks.

"It might be usual for you, but it's new to me," she said. "And I have to admit, I like it."

"Claremont growing on you, huh?" he asked.

"Yeah, it is."

The bell sounded again on the door, and this time, three families charged inside, all of them chatting about the cold and the new book club they'd heard about for their kids.

"That's a good thing," David said, "because it looks like you're going to meet the majority of the town tonight." He smiled at the new customers and at the additional families entering the bookstore behind them. "Welcome to A Likely Story!"

Chapter Seven

"I'm looking forward to meeting your friend Laura." Brother Henry shook David's hand as he exited the church Sunday morning. "Zeb told me about her moving here and working at the bookstore." He gave David a friendly smile. "That's a good thing you're doing for that young lady, giving her a place to work and helping her out when she's on her own and expecting."

"I did what any friend would do," David said.

Brother Henry nodded. "A true friend would," he agreed. "Daniel and Mandy mentioned they invited her to church this morning. Maybe she'll come worship with us eventually. We'd love to have her."

"I invited her, as well," David said. "And I'm praying she'll come, too."

"That's good. That's what works," Brother Henry answered, then turned to shake the next person's hand.

David started down the church steps with Laura

on his mind. They'd had such an amazing weekend, selling all of the *Boxcar Children* books Friday night and filling each of her sign-up sheets with kids for the book club. Thanks to Laura, the bookstore would have a record number of children in every week, and hopefully their parents would shop for books while the kids participated in the book club. His business could sure use the shot in the arm, but David wondered if it was enough.

As if he knew where David's thoughts had headed, Milton Stott waited for his client at the bottom of the steps.

"Morning, David," Milton said. "Nice service, wasn't it?"

"It was. Brother Henry always does a great job." David started toward his car and hoped that Milton wouldn't bring up business, but the accountant joined in to walk with him across the parking lot.

"David, I wanted to ask you about something I heard," he said.

Checking to make sure no one was close enough to overhear their conversation, David leaned against his car and braced for Milton's question. "Okay."

"My daughter mentioned meeting a new girl in town. Said she's expecting twins, that's she a nice lady *and* that she's working for you at the bookstore."

"She is a nice lady, a friend of mine from college, and she is expecting twins," David said. "I'd hoped to bring her to church with me this morning—maybe she'll come next week." David knew none of those things were what the accountant wanted to hear about, but he thought maybe it'd let him see that David didn't want to talk about her employment status.

Milton didn't seem to care.

"And she works for you at the bookstore?" Milton asked.

David should've known it wouldn't be that easy. "She does," he said, "and she's already brought in several new customers. We've started a book club for kids that has maxed out, and it hasn't even officially started yet. And we're expecting a large turnout for Destiny Lee's first book signing next Saturday." David attempted to control his tone so that it didn't sound like he was tossing out a sales pitch for his new employee, even if that was, for the most part, exactly what he was doing.

Milton smiled and nodded at Bo and Maura Taylor as they walked by, and David, thankful his accountant waited for them to pass before continuing this conversation, did the same. As soon as the couple got in the car next to David's and left, Milton forged ahead.

"David," he said, frowning, "I'm glad that you're making some headway in the business, and I think it's admirable that you're willing to try to help that girl out, especially given the state of your financials.

But even with those sales, I just don't see how you're going to get out of the red."

"We haven't even seen how many sales I can generate with the book signing. And the craft extravaganza is this week. That will also boost my numbers." David was grasping at straws, and the look on Milton's face said he knew it.

"Your grandmother left you two things—that bookstore and her farmhouse. The bookstore isn't making it, and every time you borrow more money against your line of credit to try to save it, you're risking losing the farmhouse, too."

When David got the line of credit and used the farmhouse as collateral, it hadn't seemed like that big of a risk. But, as Milton had pointed out, he'd been borrowing against it nearly every month in an effort to save the bookstore. Now he owed nearly as much as the place was worth, and he wasn't even living there.

"I think you need to consider two options, son. And I'm not trying to worry you. I'm just trying to save you from losing both. You need to either decide that you can make the bookstore work—somehow—and sell the farmhouse. Or you need to let the bookstore go, cut your losses and keep your grandmother's home."

"I plan to live in that house one day when I have a family," David said.

Milton grunted. "I suspected that. Well, then, I've

got to tell you, I'd recommend putting the bookstore on the market. Residential real estate isn't selling all that great now, but commercial property on the square is always a sure thing."

David's heart felt heavy in his chest. "She thought I could make the store work. I can't let her down." And he didn't want to let Laura down, either.

"Personally, I think it would've let her down more if she'd have thought you'd lose the bookstore *and* the house." Milton sighed, obviously realizing David wasn't ready to throw in the towel. "Just promise me you'll think about what I've said. It's my job to watch out for your business, and I am trying."

"I know, and I appreciate that," David said. "And I promise to think about it." He'd have no trouble keeping that promise. The fear of losing the store, and now the house, hovered in his thoughts nonstop.

"All right, then. Let me know if you need to talk."

Once Milton had left, David unlocked his door and started to get in but stopped when someone called his name.

Chad Martin had his window rolled down as he pulled up in his old BMW. "Hey, we're all heading to Stockville to try out that new Country Junction buffet. You wanna come?"

Chad's wife, Jessica, waved from the passenger seat. Their son, Nathan, sat in the backseat beside his little sister, Lainey. He also rolled his window down and told David, "I've already read up to chapter six in *The Boxcar Children.* I'll be done before our club meets."

Chad grinned. "Nathan's pretty excited about being in a club."

Jessica leaned toward her husband so that she could see David clearly and added, "We figure if he's going to join a club, a book club is a good way to go."

"Yeah, it is," David said. "So who all is going to the buffet?"

"Us, Troy and Destiny, Matt, Hannah and Autumn, Mitch and his girls, Daniel, Mandy, Kaden and Mia."

"We invited the Cutters, but Eden had already fixed lunch for all of them to eat together at her farm," Jessica said. "We're going on to the restaurant to get the table. Matt needed to run by his office on the way, and Daniel and Mandy are going by her gallery to see if the lady renting from them wants to come. Mandy said she's a friend of yours from college?"

David was thrilled they remembered Laura, and he prayed she'd come. "Yes, she is."

"So, you coming?" Chad asked.

A moment ago he was debating it, but now, the decision was easy. "Sure."

Laura still felt odd waking on a Sunday morning and not going to church. True, she'd stopped halfway through her years at UT, but she'd never gotten over that automatic impulse to get dressed, drive to the nearest church building and worship. When she first stopped, it was because none of her friends attended any service on campus and most of them—including Laura—stayed up too late on Saturday night to even consider waking up early for a church service Sunday morning.

But since she graduated, she'd thought more about church again, thought more about faith again. And nowadays, she didn't attend for totally different reasons than those in college. Now she didn't go because of guilt. She'd left God behind and ended up single and pregnant. Not only that, but she also wasn't certain parents would want her attending a worship service with their kids. What kind of example was she for teens? Then again, they might want to use her as an example of what *not* to do.

She'd eaten a bagel for breakfast, but it was nearly noon, and her stomach said the babies were hungry. She started down the stairs to the kitchen to fix a PB&J…or two…and had just peeked in the refrigerator when the back door flew open and Kaden entered.

"What ya doing? You didn't eat yet, did you? Mom said we wanted to catch you before you ate lunch, but you didn't answer your phone, so I ran in!"

"I think my phone is still by my bed upstairs," she said. "Why did you want to catch me before I ate?"

"'Cause everybody is going to the new place to eat in Stockville, and Dad and Mom wanted you to come, too. You are going to come, aren't you? 'Cause I'm hungry and we need to go."

Mandy entered the kitchen and rubbed a hand over Kaden's sandy curls. "We'd really like for you to join us," she said. "It's just a small group from church, but I'd like for you to meet them."

Laura noticed Mandy's sweaterdress, scarf and boots. Kaden wore a dark green polo shirt and khakis. She glanced down at her Titans T-shirt and maternity pajama pants. "I'm not exactly dressed for it. Maybe I'll go next time."

Mandy ran her hand down to Kaden's neck and tenderly turned him toward the door. "Kaden, go on and tell your daddy that we'll be out in a minute. We need to give Laura a second to change."

"But—" Laura began.

Neither listened.

"Okay!" Kaden ran to the door, leaped from the top stair to the pavement and then continued to their minivan shouting to his father that Laura was coming.

Mandy crossed the room, took Laura's hand from the refrigerator handle and then eased the door shut. "I want you to go. You've been either working at the bookstore or cooped up in here all week. You need to get out, and I want you to meet our friends."

"Your *church* friends," Laura said.

"Same difference."

"I don't belong with a church group now. It doesn't feel right for me to go. After I have the babies, I plan to start back. I want them to grow up knowing God, but now..."

"Now is the perfect time for you to start back."

"I've made so many mistakes. Mistakes that are—" she glanced at her growing stomach "—rather obvious." Then she thought about how that sounded and said, "I don't mean that my babies are a mistake. I'm excited about having them and hopeful that I'll do a good job as a new mom."

"I believe you will," Mandy interjected.

"But," Laura continued, "I'm afraid people will look at me and feel like I shouldn't be in church."

"Maybe *you* don't feel like you should be, but I think people will surprise you. Come eat lunch with us today," Mandy said. "You need to meet some of the folks that you think won't want you in church. Then tell me what you think. And besides, I have something to talk to you about over lunch. Another book club idea for the bookstore."

"Couldn't we talk about it here?" Laura asked.

"Nope. Now get dressed, please. I'm hungry." Mandy smiled and pointed to the stairs. "Go on."

"Are you always this bossy?"

"That's a question for my husband," she answered with a laugh.

Laura went to her room and changed into one of

the new outfits her mother had brought. The mocha color-block dress had zigzagging diagonal stripes of chocolate and red accenting the skirt and flowed beautifully to Laura's ankles. She added the red jewelry her mother had bought to match the dress and chocolate flats. After running a brush through her hair and putting on a little mascara and lip gloss, she grabbed her purse and phone.

Before leaving, she took a final glance in the mirror. She still wasn't used to the new shape of her body, but even so, she did think pregnancy agreed with her. Her cheeks were rosy without blush, and her hair was healthier, too, probably due to the prenatal vitamins. Wearing the maternity clothes was also fun, especially when she had so many to choose from, thanks to her mom. She thought of her mom and sure hoped her dad would be able to help Laura figure out what was wrong. Laura looked forward to his visit after Thanksgiving.

She ran her hand along the fabric covering her stomach and smiled when one of the girls kicked toward her palm. "Don't worry. I'm feeding you soon." Then she left to join her friends in the van.

Mia was in her car seat in the middle section, a pacifier in her mouth. Kaden sat buckled in the very back.

"Wow, you look really pretty!" he said as Laura climbed in.

"That's my boy," Daniel said from the driver's seat. "Already knows how to compliment the ladies."

Mandy laughed, and Laura grinned. "Well, thank you, Kaden. You just made my day."

"Cool!"

"You do look very nice," Mandy agreed, "and we're glad you decided to come."

"Me, too," Laura admitted. It did feel good to get out with friends, and she found herself looking forward to meeting the others at the restaurant. She'd met quite a few of Claremont's residents over the past week and with each person she met, she grew a little fonder of her new town. It seemed the perfect place to raise her girls.

Her phone buzzed in her purse and she withdrew it to see she'd missed three messages. The first two were from Mandy.

Mandy Brantley: Hey, we're leaving church now. Want to come get you to go eat. Okay?

Mandy Brantley: Didn't hear back from you but we're on our way anyway ;) We want you to meet our friends.

She smiled at Mandy's persistence and then noticed that the third message was from David. She opened it.

David Presley: Mandy is inviting you to lunch. Say yes. See you there.

Laura hadn't known that David was part of the group going to lunch. She fiddled with the red beads on her necklace and wondered if, like Kaden, David might think she looked pretty, too.

During the twenty-minute drive to Stockville, Kaden told her all about everything he already liked about *The Boxcar Children* and how he had read more than any of the other kids in his class, but that he wouldn't tell what happened before they got to it. And while she listened to Kaden, she entertained Mia.

The baby withdrew her pacifier, tiny lips smacking with the action, tossed it in Laura's lap and giggled.

"Binky," she said, reaching for it.

Laura handed it back, and Mia proceeded to toss it again, her blue eyes glittering with mischief.

After the third toss, Laura realized the game wasn't ending, and she didn't care. To hear that baby belly laugh warmed her heart.

"She's got your number," Mandy said, looking around her seat to see her little princess. "Don't you." She squeezed Mia's knee, and the baby laughed even harder.

By the time they got to Stockville, Laura had

retrieved Mia's binky at least a couple dozen times. Her own babies were restless in her tummy, and Laura wondered what it'd be like to hear her little girls laugh the way Mia laughed now. She couldn't wait.

She walked behind Daniel and Mandy as they entered the restaurant. Daniel carried Mia and snagged a high chair as he headed toward a long table with several people already seated. "We brought Miss Laura!" Kaden announced.

Everyone said hello, and Mandy performed a quick introduction. "Laura, this is Mitch Gillespie and his daughters, Dee and Emmie." Mitch had reddish hair and a nice smile, reminding Laura of Prince Harry. Dee and Emmie both had strawberry curls, with Dee looking to be around two or three and Emmie about the same age as Mia.

"Nice to meet you," she said.

Mitch unwrapped a pack of crackers for Emmie and placed a few on her high-chair tray. "You, too," he said.

Daniel put Mia in a high chair next to Emmie's, and the two immediately started chattering and eating the crackers.

"And this is Dr. Matt Graham. You already met his wife, Hannah, and daughter, Autumn," Mandy said. "Then there's Troy and Destiny Lee. Destiny is our new local author and will be doing the book signing at A Likely Story next Saturday."

"Nice to meet you," Laura said, and then turned to the only person Mandy hadn't yet introduced.

"And of course you know David," Mandy said, grinning. "So, who wants to head to the buffet?"

Everyone answered in agreement and started toward the long tables of food in the center of the restaurant. Everyone, that is, except for the man wearing a black cashmere sweater over a pale blue polo shirt and black dress pants. The guy whose cologne again teased her senses because he stood so near. Her friend. Her employer. And right now, the guy making her heart beat so hard it was probably deafening her children.

Laura did not want to have a relationship again. Not yet. So why did every ounce of her being act like she wanted one now? Right here. Right now. She licked her lips and wondered what to say and whether he was thinking anything at all like what she was thinking.

He moved even closer, brought his mouth near her left ear and said, "You look amazing." His warm breath against her neck sent a patch of goose bumps down her arm, and she was thankful that the new dress had long sleeves.

"Thanks."

"I'm glad you came," he said.

She smiled. "Me, too."

"Y'all coming, or not?" Kaden called from the line by the food.

"We're coming." David waved a hand in front of her. "Ladies first."

Her stomach growled loudly, and she laughed. "And it's a good thing, because these ladies are hungry."

Laura filled her plate with roast beef, black-eyed peas, turnip greens and cornbread. David went for the meat loaf, potatoes, sweet peas and a roll.

Returning to the table, Daniel offered grace and they began eating, the kids chattering noisily and the adults talking about the delicious food, which Hannah described as "good ol' family-reunion-style cooking." Laura had never had enough family to have a family reunion, but she imagined if she did, it would be something like this. Everyone eating and laughing and chatting. They treated Laura as if she belonged here, with all of them, regardless of the fact that they'd all attended church this morning and she'd stayed home. Not once did anyone ask anything about the father of her children or why she was on her own. In fact, the only questions they asked were ones that would allow them to get to know her better...and even help her out.

"So, if you're going to keep working after the babies are born, have you found a place for them to stay?" Jessica asked between bites of chicken and dumplings. "Because I work at the Claremont day care, and I have to say, we have an amazing nursery program."

"You'd say all of your programs are amazing, wouldn't you?" her husband asked.

She took another bite, grinned. "It's the truth."

"She's right, the day care is top-notch," Hannah said. "I decided to stay home with Autumn, but if I did send my kids anywhere, that's where they'd go."

"I haven't decided what I'm doing yet," Laura said honestly. She had planned to look and see what was available, but since she'd only been in Claremont for a week, she hadn't had a chance. "I hope to spend a few weeks with them before I have to take them anywhere." She hadn't asked David about that, and she also wasn't sure how she'd stay with her girls if she wasn't working.

Suddenly her meal didn't look as appealing, and her stomach churned for another reason. What if she couldn't afford to spend a little time with the girls before going back to work? And how hard would it be to leave them if they were merely weeks old? Then another worry—how would she afford to pay for day care?

The majority of the table moved ahead with conversation, but David, sitting in the next chair, leaned toward Laura. "I don't have a problem with you bringing them to the bookstore. We'll work it out."

And just like that, her worries eased up a little. She still knew that she'd need to find something for the girls eventually, but if he'd let her start out bringing them with her to the bookstore, that would help. "Thank you," she whispered.

"Don't worry," he said.

She couldn't make that promise, because even now, she continued to think of her concerns, but she smiled, nodded and began to eat again.

"I wanted to talk to both of you about a book club for women that I'd like y'all to start at the bookstore. I think it'd be very popular, and I know it'd be beneficial to all of us," Mandy said. "Daniel has recommended the women at church spending more time together away from the regular church services, and I agree that it's a great idea. I was thinking about a book club that focused on women of the Bible, specifically the women in the lineage of Christ."

"Oh, I've seen those books, the series, I mean. Is that what you're talking about?" Destiny asked. "It starts with Tamar, then Rahab, Ruth, Bathsheba and Mary, right?"

Mandy nodded. "That's the one. David, it's called *The Lineage of Grace*. Could you order those for us? And Laura, do you think you could kind of lead us in the book club? I think there are study questions we could use, but I'll admit that I've never been in a book club before."

"I can order the books tomorrow," David said.

"And I'd be happy to help lead it," Laura said, excited that they were starting yet another book club to help David's store. "When were y'all thinking you'd want to meet?"

"Maybe Tuesday evenings?" Mandy said. "How about seven-thirty, so we'd have time to get the kids fed and done with homework and all. Would that work?"

"That's after the bookstore closes, but I think after hours for the adult book clubs would be better anyway. Less interruptions. It sounds great." Laura's appetite had completely returned now, and she turned her attention back to the delicious roast and gravy. She also found herself easily chatting with the others at the table and could tell that no one seemed to think any less of her or judge her or...anything. In fact, she realized that the "church friends" weren't so bad.

Maybe, with David's encouragement and with the friendships that she'd begun to develop with those seated at this table, she might actually find her way back to church again, too.

Chapter Eight

David's store was more packed than it'd ever been, with parents browsing—and buying—while their kids were busy enjoying the book club with Laura. He stayed attuned to his customers' needs but also peeked at what was happening in the children's area at every opportunity.

"I could totally live in a boxcar," Kaden said. "I like these berries a lot." He popped another couple of blueberries in his mouth and grinned at Laura, who proceeded to explain that the kids in the book didn't only live on berries. Then she also reminded Kaden of how good he had it to be able to live with his parents.

"Yeah, I know," Kaden said, "but still, I think I'm gonna ask Mom to get us lots of berries from the grocery. I do really like 'em."

The other kids in the group joined in with their comments of berries, questions about the children in the book and about boxcars in general.

"This is wonderful for Kaden," Mandy said as she moved to stand near David and see the interaction. "For all of the kids really." Then she lowered her voice and added, "And it's good for Laura, too, don't you think?"

"I do," he agreed. Indeed, Laura had been just as excited, or maybe even more, than the children about beginning the book club this week. Tonight was only the second night, but both evenings had filled the bookstore and also had the kids talking about looking forward to their next meeting. Consequently, David had his highest weekday sales ever.

"She showed me some pamphlets she printed out online about the train station in Stockville. Said she wanted to take the children on a field trip in the spring to look at real boxcars."

"I know. She mentioned that to me yesterday, and I think it's a great idea," David said, liking the notion of Laura still being here in the spring and praying his business continued to pick up so he could ensure that they still had a bookstore to run.

"She'd be a great schoolteacher," Mandy said, "but I can't help but think she's also very good at what she does here. I can't see her doing both, but if she does eventually take a job in the school system, maybe you could find someone else for this position?"

"Maybe so," David said, but he felt the same as Mandy; Laura was perfect for the bookstore. "Or maybe she'd decide to just work here." If he could pay her.

Mandy nudged him with her shoulder. "That's what I'm talking about."

David knew it was a long shot, but he thought it would be wonderful if the bookstore could eventually hold its own.

"So did those books for the women's book club come in yet?" Mandy asked. "I was hoping to get started on the first one."

"They'll be here tomorrow."

"Awesome. I'll pick them up and hand them out to everyone at church tomorrow night." She looked again at Laura. "Think she'd want to come to church with us for the midweek study?"

"I asked, and she said she still didn't think she was ready. But it wouldn't hurt for you to ask, too." He loved it that Mandy and several others in town had taken an interest in Laura, not only personally but also spiritually. She had that quality, the ability to draw you in and make you care about her, probably because she cared so much for others. Now, in fact, she'd taken little Savannah Jameson in her lap and was letting her help turn the pages in the book.

"Look at that, isn't that precious," Mandy said, watching Savannah's eyes widen as she looked up at Laura telling the story. The little girl turned the page and then moved her hand to rest on Laura's tummy. "Hold these books," Mandy said, passing the stack in her arms to David. "I've got my camera in my purse."

David took the books and watched as Mandy quietly got her camera ready then raised it to take several pictures of Laura surrounded by the children. Laura was so into the discussion that she didn't notice.

"It's moments like that you can't get in a studio," Mandy said. "I'm predicting that will be a gallery favorite."

"I'd like a copy," David said, then when Mandy smiled knowingly, he added, "for the bookstore. It'll be good for customers to see the book club in action."

"Uh-huh," Mandy said, still grinning, but David didn't acknowledge anything. Laura didn't feel that way about him; she never had, or she'd have noticed his attention when they first met back in college instead of zeroing in on Jared. And the next time David had a relationship, he wanted someone who wanted *him*.

"You ready for me to ring you up?" He indicated the books balanced in his arms.

"Sure." Mandy obviously decided to drop her suspicions for now, and he was grateful. He didn't need all of the customers browsing the bookstore to think there was something going on between him and his employee.

They moved to the checkout counter and David

took her payment while Titus Jameson stood nearby. Mandy paid, said hello to Titus and then returned to the children's reading area to continue watching Kaden and the other kids.

"Anything I can help you find, Titus?" David asked.

"No, I just wanted to thank you for this book club that you've started. Savannah, well, she loves reading, but she hasn't seemed to enjoy it as much ever since her mom left." He nodded toward the big boxcar prop and all of the children sitting around it. "She's really taken to this story and to Laura." His mouth flattened, and David could tell the guy was holding back on his emotions. Titus was only a couple of years older than David, but he'd been through a lot this year with his wife leaving him for someone else and then heading out of town with the new guy. From what David had heard, she hadn't even seen Savannah since she left.

David swallowed past his own emotions and said, "Well, it looks like Laura has taken to Savannah, too."

Titus nodded. "I can see that, and I appreciate it more than you could know." He ran a hand across his chin and said, "Something else, David."

"What's that?"

"Business has been down, you know. Not a lot of people building right now with the economy the way it is." Titus owned the only construction company in town and had always seemed to do very well with his business, but David hadn't seen any new houses going up lately or renovations, for that matter. "I was wondering," Titus continued, "if you might have any work you'd like to get done."

David shook his head. "I wish I could help you," he said. "The truth is that I am wanting to make some changes to one of the rooms in my apartment upstairs, but I was thinking my dad and I would work on that when he's here for Thanksgiving."

"I understand," Titus said solemnly.

"The thing is, I'd much rather hire someone to do it, and for that matter, I'd love to hire someone to fix up the old farmhouse I inherited from my grandmother. It needs, well, pretty much everything. But I just can't do it right now." He didn't explain that the economy was also killing him, but Titus's knowing nod said he understood.

"No problem," he said. "Something will work out. Hey, could I put a couple of flyers up in your window? Maybe someone needs work done. It's getting close to Christmas, you know, and I want Savannah to have a good one, especially with everything she's been through this year."

"Sure."

"I'll go get a couple from my truck and put them up tonight if that's okay."

"That's fine," David said, "and if I hear of anyone needing work done, I'll tell them to call you."

"I'd appreciate that," Titus said.

"I'll do the same." Zeb Shackleford had moved to the counter with a small stack of books and heard the last of their conversation.

Titus gave the older man a smile. "Thank you, Zeb."

Zeb's mouth slid to the side as he watched Titus make his way out of the store. "That boy's had a tough year."

"I know. I wish I could help him out," David said.

"I know you do," Zeb said.

David looked at the four books Zeb had on the counter and watched the man withdraw his worn wallet. He quietly whispered, "Don't. I'm not taking it."

Zeb whispered back, "One day, I'm repaying you." He pointed to David. "You can count on it. Somehow, I will."

"Laura said you were going to repay us by letting us go with you for some of your visits to read to the kids."

Zeb's face split into a smile and sent his wrinkles branching in all new directions. "I was going to ask y'all about that tonight. I know you're busy this month with the extravaganza, Destiny's book signing, Thanksgiving and all. Hoping y'all will be real busy for Black Friday."

"Me, too," David said.

"But how about in December y'all can come with

me to the hospital? I try to go each night that month, since the kids are thinking about Christmas and all. It's easy for them to get sad during the holidays." He shrugged. "I try to help 'em stay happy."

"That sounds great," David said.

"Good deal." Zeb took his books off the counter. "Tell Laura I said good-night. I'm heading home."

"I will."

Laura loved every minute of her time with the kids and also enjoyed chancing a glance at David every now and again to see him smiling, obviously thrilled with the customers filling his store. When the book club hour ended, she found that the kids lingered, wanting to talk to her more about Henry, Violet, Jessie and Benny, the four children in the story. Laura was especially taken with Savannah Jameson. The little girl continued to ask questions about Violet and seemed to drink in every word. Laura had dreamed of teaching children who were that eager to learn, and it was just as wonderful as she'd thought it would be.

By the time they were down to the last customer, it was ten minutes past closing time. The pretty lady lingered at the doorway chatting with David while Laura tidied up the children's area and tried not to look overly interested in the fact that they were talking. The woman's name was Haley Calhoun, and Laura had learned that she was one of the two town vets. Haley had stopped by to pick up a couple of books David had ordered her about quarter horses, and she was nice to Laura, but in Laura's opinion, she was a bit nicer to David. She talked about church and about the fact that she thought David should have a puppy or a kitten in the bookstore, and Laura couldn't help but notice that she and David seemed to get along very well. And they looked good together, too.

Haley wore a fitted white jacket, black riding pants and black boots. She'd explained that she'd come straight from riding because she'd remembered that the bookstore closed at 6:00 p.m. The fact that she looked absolutely stunning in her riding gear only added to Laura's discomfort at watching her stick around and talk to David.

David laughed at something she said, and Laura did a one-eighty to keep from staring and dropping her jaw. Instead she moved as far away from the front of the store as possible and checked the author names for alphabetization.

She hardly paid attention to the books, however, because she was too busy silently chastising herself. She *wanted* David to be interested in someone. She didn't want to have a relationship herself, so why should she care that he was showing another female attention? She shouldn't.

Moving from the A's to the B's, she caught sight of a C book, yanked it out, found the correct location and jabbed it into place with as much force as she could muster.

"Easy there, slugger. They tend to sell better if they are still in one piece."

She'd been so absorbed in her thoughts/jealousy/whatever that she hadn't heard him *finally* tell Haley goodbye. Her cheeks flamed and from the way his brows lifted and his glasses followed suit, he could tell.

"You upset about something?"

"No, of course not." She forced a laugh. "I'm just happy that everything went so well tonight, aren't you?" Did that sound *too* enthusiastic? Because she was happy, but she was also angry, and she wasn't about to admit why.

"I am. Best sales night on a weekday ever, excluding holidays," he said, reaching past her to push another book in place. His arm brushed her side, and Laura fought the urge to lean into it.

These hormones were getting the best of her. She needed David to be dating someone so he'd officially be off-limits and stop messing with her head.

"Why aren't you dating anyone?" she blurted and then wished that she could push the words back in. But the widening of his eyes and the slight drop in his jaw said that there was no going back now. He'd heard what was on her mind, and he looked…more than a little surprised. Well, Laura had lost some of her filter for saying what was on her mind over the past few months. Maybe it *was* the pregnancy hormones in action, or maybe it was simply the fact that she didn't understand the bizarreness of her old friend, her attractive and kind and nice—okay, a little more gorgeous than she remembered—old friend being *so* single.

When he didn't readily offer a response, Laura, being Laura, couldn't stand the silence and decided to fill the vacant air with words. "You're a good-looking guy, you own your own business—" granted, it wasn't anywhere near what one would consider a thriving business, but Laura was in the process of fixing that "—you're nice to an extreme, honest to a fault..." She paused because the look on his face had shifted from surprise...to shock. "I just don't get it," she continued. "Several of the girls—women—who've been in the shop this week are interested in you. I'm pretty sure the one that just left could also be counted in that number. I don't know how you can't see it. I mean, do you want me to kind of, I don't know, find out if they want to go out with you or something?" At the moment, the thought of fixing David up didn't sound so appealing, but it'd sure help ease the tension between the two of them and control some of this infatuation she'd suddenly discovered toward her old friend.

His brows dipped, and he looked as though he were holding back a laugh. "I appreciate the offer," he said, "but to be completely honest, I think I have already been out with every single lady that visited the store this week."

That wasn't what she expected. "You have?"

He set that laugh free. "Don't sound so surprised."

"No, I didn't mean it like that," she said, then frowned. How did she mean it? "Well, then, why aren't you dating any of them, like, seriously?"

"Because I haven't felt *seriously* about any of them," he said, as though this conversation had run its course.

Laura didn't think it had. "But you like dating one person. You liked being serious," she said, recalling how committed he was to his girlfriend in college. "You dated Cassadee nearly two years when we were at UT." Then Laura recalled the reason they'd broken up. David had returned home to Claremont for Mia's funeral, started thinking about life and religion and all of the other things that come to mind after the loss of a loved one, and then he decided he had messed up by letting his faith go in college. "You two broke up because she didn't share your faith." She glanced up at him. "Is that why you haven't gotten serious with the girls you've dated here? Because they don't share your faith?"

"I only went out with the ones that do share my faith," he said, "but the truth is, I didn't feel 'that way' about them. Sharing faith is important to me, but you need..." He appeared to search for the word and then said, "You need more."

Laura knew what "more" he referred to. Attraction, that spark that simply happens when two people are together and know that they could have something special. *That* was what he meant. And unfortunately, Laura was pretty sure *that* was exactly what she was beginning to feel. But fortunately, the other statement he made reminded her that even if she did want any type of relationship, it would never happen with David.

I only went out with the ones that do share my faith.

And that eliminated Laura from any equation involving David. Twice he'd asked her if she wanted to join him at church, and twice she'd declined. And he'd already invited her to tomorrow night's midweek worship, and already, she'd declined. Not necessarily because she didn't share his faith, but because she still wasn't certain she'd be welcomed there. She'd been able to handle the lunch last Sunday with Mandy's friends, but she still felt like too much of a hypocrite to go and mingle with the real Christians full-time.

Laura realized she'd been sitting silently while he waited for her next question. And she felt a little badly for the bold interrogation regarding his dating habits. "Sorry, I was being nosy."

"Sometimes that's what friends do, right?" He leaned against the bookshelves and looked mighty nice doing it. "We are still friends, aren't we, Laura?

Or…are we something else?" His eyes were so focused on her hers that Laura felt her breath catch. And she noticed that they weren't merely brown; they were chocolate. With tiny gold flecks near the center. They were exquisite, and she found that she couldn't stop looking at them. "Laura?" he prodded.

She didn't want a relationship. She didn't. She'd made a conscious decision that she wouldn't pursue anyone, or allow anyone to pursue her, which, of course, David wasn't doing. At all. So she should be happy, ecstatic even. Why had she even brought up this whole "why aren't you dating?" thing? And why had she gotten so jealous when she saw him talking to Haley Calhoun?

Uncomfortable with the fact that her emotions were trying to trump her mind, she took a step back, bumped her behind against a bookshelf and managed a smile. "We're still friends," she said, then she promptly turned away from those knowing eyes and made a beeline for home.

Chapter Nine

David rang up sale after sale as the entire Claremont community, as well as those from the surrounding counties, lined up for their autographed copies of *Southern Love in Claremont.* With Destiny Lee featuring over fifty Claremont love stories, practically everyone knew someone in the book. Luckily for David, it appeared everyone who was in the book or knew someone in the book wanted a copy or two.

By the end of the night, he'd sold all but twenty copies.

"Wow," Destiny said, beaming as she capped her pen, "that was incredible."

"I'll say it was," Troy said, undeniably happy for his wife. "You were awesome."

"And you were awesome, Laura," Destiny said as Laura picked up the empty plates and bottles around the signing area. "I hadn't considered having anything for them to snack on while they waited. Those cookies were a hit, and the bottled water kept them happy, too."

"I read up on how to have a successful book signing," Laura said. "The number-one thing the sites recommended was plenty of snacks and water."

"Well, it worked," Destiny said.

David joined Laura in picking up the trash. She seemed to notice he was helping but didn't look in his direction. She'd avoided eye contact like the plague since her questions about his dating status on Tuesday; however, David had felt her gaze on more than one occasion.

He reached for an empty water bottle at the same time that Laura noticed it, and their hands collided on the plastic. David didn't move his, but she jerked hers away as though she'd been scalded.

He smiled. She blushed. And David wondered what was happening between himself and his new employee.

Destiny cleared her throat, and David knew by looking at the lady that she'd seen the odd reaction. Then she laughed out loud.

Laura looked up. "Everything okay?"

Troy put his arm around his wife. "Yeah," Troy said, apparently watching everything, "my wife is just happy. I think I'll take her out to dinner to celebrate. How about Messina's?"

"Sounds yummy." Destiny gave David and Laura

a finger wave. "Y'all have a great night, and thanks again."

"You're welcome," they both said, and then continued cleaning up while the couple left the bookstore.

After tossing the last paper plate in the trash, Laura walked behind the counter to get her purse. The past three nights, David let her say her quick goodbye and rush to exit. But he didn't feel like letting her run away again tonight. He moved to stand between the end of the counter and the wall, essentially blocking her in. "Where are you headed?"

She slid the strap of her purse a little higher on her shoulder and then ran her fingers across the beads of her necklace. "Just going on home to eat and go to sleep. Been a long day." She took a small step toward him and waited for him to move.

David didn't budge. Her hand continued flitting across the red and gold beads of the long necklace. She looked beautiful, as always, wearing a long black dress that nearly met the floor, a red jacket and red and gold dangly earrings that matched her necklace. Red flat shoes similar to ballerina slippers peeked beneath the hem of her dress.

"Excuse me, please." She attempted another step, and again he stood his ground.

"I'm not letting you go home before we celebrate."

Her eyes widened, and her mouth opened in a

little *O*. Then she cleared her throat and asked, "Celebrate? Celebrate what?"

"This was the best sales night in the history of the bookstore, or at least as long as I've owned it," he said. "If that doesn't call for a celebration, I don't know what does."

She seemed to consider his invitation but then shook her head. "I really do need to get home. It's been a long day, and I think I'll just eat a sandwich and go on to bed."

"All right then," he said. "Coffee and a sandwich it is." He turned and waved her through the opening to exit the counter area.

"Coffee and a sandwich?" she asked, and he was glad to see she appeared to be holding back a smile.

"Have you been to The Grind yet? It's delicious."

"The coffee shop? No," she said. "Do they have more than coffee? I mean, I like coffee, even if I'm only drinking decaffeinated now for the babies, but you said coffee and a sandwich."

"Reubens, turkey and brie, roast beef, pecan chicken salad, BLT with applewood bacon." He took a breath to keep going, but she held up a hand.

"You had me at turkey and brie."

He laughed and was pleased to see her join in. She'd been nervous and jittery around him ever since their awkward conversation Tuesday night, when she'd shocked him by showing a hint of jealousy. The emotion didn't coincide with the type of relationship he'd believed they had, and if she were jealous…what did that mean? Was Laura actually feeling something toward him beyond friend and employer?

"So, sandwich and coffee with the boss," she said, stepping ahead of him toward the door, "to celebrate our big night."

David was pretty sure she clarified because she didn't want this to appear like a date. Which was fine. He didn't, either. He simply wanted to celebrate, and he also wasn't quite ready to send Laura home.

Fifteen minutes later, they were seated at one of the cozy bistro tables near the fireplace inside The Grind sipping on vanilla lattes and listening to the band More Than This playing contemporary Christian music. Laura ordered the turkey and brie, of course, and David had his traditional Reuben. Both had the homemade sweet potato chips on the side.

Laura hummed her contentment through the first bite, and David nodded.

"Told you it was good."

"You were telling the truth," she said.

"I always try to."

The band finished playing "Lifted High" and then went to take a break. David and Laura clapped along with the others in the coffee house.

"They're really good," she said.

"I know. It's amazing how much talent we have locally, for a town this small."

She took another bite of her sandwich and hummed again.

He grinned, and she blushed.

"Sorry. It's just *so* good."

"I'm glad you're enjoying it," he said, "and I'm glad you agreed to come out with me."

Her eyes widened as she chewed, then she tapped beneath her throat as she swallowed. "But—this isn't a date," she said, "is it?"

David shook his head. "Just a celebration."

"I knew that." She took another bite, smiling through her chewing.

"I hope you know how much I appreciate everything you've done at the store this week. The book club is a hit, and the signing today was so much better because of you. Destiny was right—you did a great job keeping the crowd happy while they waited."

"It only took a few searches on the internet," she said, plucking a sweet potato chip from her plate and taking a bite.

"But you took the time to do it, and it worked. I appreciate that."

She ate another chip. "Hence our celebration."

"Exactly." He polished off his sandwich and then listened to the band tune their instruments to get ready for another song. Soon they'd started into "Where You Are," and David softly sang along.

When the song ended, he turned to see Laura had finished everything on her plate and was looking at him with a strange expression.

"What?" he asked.

"You sing, too. Is there anything you can't do?"

"I told you before, I can't cook, nothing more than eggs and anything grilled. I'm fairly hopeless in the kitchen."

"Sure you are," she said, tossing her napkin on the table.

Grinning, David caught the attention of their waitress. "Rhonda, which cookies do you have fresh out of the oven?"

"They just finished making the white-chocolate macadamia-nut cookies," she said.

"Awesome. We'll take four cookies and two lattes to go please, and the check."

She pulled her notepad out of her pocket, jotted down the additional items and handed him the ticket. "There you go. I'll be right back with your cookies and lattes."

"What if I don't want cookies?" Laura asked.

"Then there will be more for me," David said. "You don't want warm, gooey, fresh-out-of-the-oven white-chocolate macadamia-nut cookies?"

She smirked. "You know I do."

"That's what I thought," he said.

Rhonda returned, placed the cups on the table and handed David a small white bag that smelled incredible. He thanked her, paid her and then asked Laura, "Ready to go?"

Laura couldn't remember ever feeling quite this special. David opened the door for her as they left the coffee house, and she worked to pull her jacket tighter with her free hand. David noticed and reached for her cup.

"Let me hold it while you tighten your coat," he said, his fingers grazing hers as he wrapped them around the cup and slid it away.

Laura attempted to ignore the sensation that zinged through her at the mere contact, drew her jacket closer around her and tightened the belt. "Thanks," she said, reaching for the coffee, their fingers brushing again with the exchange.

"Just wait until you try this." He withdrew a steaming cookie from the bag.

Laura reached for the treat, but it was so warm and gooey that it bent in half and broke, the majority of it landing with a plop on the sidewalk.

"No way," David said, frowning.

Laura looked at the goo on the sidewalk and the disappointment on his face and burst out laughing.

"Hey now, this isn't funny." He still had a small dab of cookie in his fingers, and it appeared to be melting to the touch.

"Oh, I beg to differ," she said, laughing so hard she nearly spilled her coffee, "it's very funny."

Obviously seeing what happened, Rhonda darted out of the restaurant with enough napkins to choke a horse and shoved them at David. "Here you go!" she said.

Which only made Laura laugh harder. And even though her coffee had a lid, it still sloshed through the drink hole, and for some reason, she found that quite hysterical, too.

David used a napkin to get the mess off the sidewalk, tossed it in a nearby can and then made another effort to pull a cookie from the sack, this time with a napkin.

He handed the napkin-encased cookie to Laura and she happily took a bite.

The sweet white chocolate melted on her tongue. "Oh, wow, you were right. These are amazing."

"Thanks," Rhonda said, then she headed back into the coffee house.

David and Laura started walking down the sidewalk, and he pulled another cookie from the bag. It started folding over, and this time, he tossed the whole thing in his mouth.

"Kinda hard to take your time enjoying it that way, isn't it?" she asked.

He smirked. "Oh, I enjoyed it."

They neared Carter Photography, and she glanced

at the white sack. "Okay, I'm ready for my other one," she said.

He grinned. "Your other one was the one I dropped on the sidewalk. This one's mine." He lifted the last cookie, which, maybe because it'd had a little time to cool, stayed together.

"Hey, I'm eating for three here," she said.

"You have a point." He handed her the cookie.

Laura propped her coffee in the crook of her arm so she could break the cookie in half, then handed part to David. "Here."

He took it. "You sure?" he asked, tossing it in his mouth.

She laughed. "Well, I guess I'd better be, huh?"

"Looks that way."

She ate the last bite of hers. "Thanks for the celebration dinner and for walking me home."

"You're welcome." He stepped beneath the awning and watched as she found her keys in her purse and then moved to unlock the door. "I'll make sure you get inside safely."

Laura nodded and fumbled to slide the key into the lock. Finally, it clicked, and she turned the knob. It almost felt like the end of a date, like the moment when she'd stall, hold her breath and wait for their first kiss. She looked back at the man who'd already touched her heart in ways that no one else ever had. "But this isn't a date?" She'd meant it to come out as a statement, but the question was there, just the same. Why couldn't she stop her mouth from blurting whatever traipsed across her heart? She was practically *asking* for this to be a date, and that wasn't what she wanted.

Remember Jared. Remember how much relationships hurt. Remember how you promised—promised—*yourself that you would not jump into another one too soon!*

But this is David. He's perfect, her heart whispered, and her mind quickly screamed, *You thought Jared was perfect, too!*

He stepped closer, and Laura braced for a kiss that she was pretty sure would rock her to her toes. A kiss she did *not* want. Really.

"This isn't a date," he whispered.

Stunned, she blinked, nodded. "Have a good night," she said, opening the door.

"And, Laura..."

She looked back into those dark eyes, at the gold flecks catching the porch light. "Yes?"

"If I took you on a date, you wouldn't have to ask. You'd know."

Chapter Ten

Laura set aside Sunday to read the remainder of Destiny's book and to get started on the Tamar novel that the women's book club would discuss on Tuesday evening. With the past two weeks being so busy, she hadn't been able to read more than a couple of the love stories in Destiny's book, but she was already hooked. She fixed a cup of coffee, grabbed a quilt and the book then headed out to the balcony to read.

Most all of the apartments on the square had balconies overlooking the center area, where the three-tiered fountain flowed and a few geese ambled around the wrought-iron benches, where the elderly typically sat with bread. But unlike every other morning of the week, today the square was primarily empty, probably because people were home getting ready for church.

Laura assumed everyone she went to lunch with last Sunday would gather at the Claremont Community Church today, as would David.

She sipped her oversize mug of coffee. The crisp taste instantly reminded her of the lattes she'd shared with him a week ago and that parting comment that had teased her ever since.

She'd hardly been able to sleep for remembering his words and wondering what it would be like to go on a real date with David Presley.

A shiver passed over her, and it had nothing to do with the cold. She focused on the book and tried to tune out the memory of how badly she'd wanted to be kissed. And how he hadn't even tried. She turned the page and attempted to focus on the next story. It was interesting to read about couples she'd already met in town.

The first story was about Marvin and Mae Tolleson, the older couple who owned the variety store. And she'd read about Mandy and Daniel, learned how they'd started out basically despising one another because both of them wanted to adopt Kaden when his parents passed away. This morning she started into the third story, about Chad and Jessica. Soaking in the pages, Laura learned that Jessica was pregnant with Chad's baby when she ran away from Claremont as a teen, and she didn't tell him for six years. The story of how they reunited and how he forgave her for leaving touched Laura's heart. She thought of adorable little Nathan in the book club and realized that he was that precious baby who finally met his daddy.

Tears trickled down Laura's cheeks. Her little girls would never have a relationship with their biological father. Jared had made certain she knew that he didn't want any part of this pregnancy or their lives. But Laura wanted them to have a daddy, eventually.

A steady thumping caught her attention. She wiped the tears away and looked for the source of the noise, growing louder. Then she saw the jogger entering the square from Main Street. David ran steadily down the sidewalk, his tennis shoes producing the pounding she'd heard. Oddly, the even thudding of his shoes reminded her of the sounds she heard at each doctor's visit, her babies' heartbeats.

Laura's heart kicked it up a notch, too. He wore a gray T-shirt and navy sweatpants. An iPod was strapped around his right bicep with a white cord connecting the earphones. His shirt wasn't overly tight, but it still managed to emphasize the hard planes of his chest, flexing and releasing with each breath.

She continued staring until he reached the bookstore. He held one hand out to brace against the brick wall and checked his watch. Then he nodded, apparently satisfied with his time. He pulled the earphones out and then started to go into the store but, to Laura's surprise, he tossed a glance over his shoulder, locked eyes with her and smiled.

She should have waved, or yelled hello, or *something*. But instead she clutched the book, gathered the quilt and the coffee and retreated inside. She glanced at her closet. Several dresses hung there that would be perfect to wear to church today. A tiny whisper told her to get dressed and go. But while that voice whispered, her fear screamed louder. What if Mandy's friends weren't typical, and the remainder of the people there would rather a single, very pregnant lady not show up in the middle of their small community church? Laura couldn't deny she was starting to have serious feelings toward David, and he wanted—needed—a woman who shared his faith. If he'd have patience, Laura would get there again. As soon as she thought God was ready for her. She figured He'd let her know somehow when the time was right.

"So, did you finish reading the book?" Hannah asked Mandy as they each plopped down in one of the cozy chairs at the front of the bookstore.

"I read it in two days," Mandy said, placing a hand over her heart. "It was amazing."

"I have to admit that I'd never really thought about the story from Tamar's point of view, and I found myself rooting for her more than any character I've ever read about," Hannah said.

Several more ladies came in and filled the chairs and sofas that David had arranged for the night's meeting. Laura said hello to Destiny and Jessica and met a sweet older lady named Mary, who said she was married to the preacher at the church. Then Eden Sanders came in and introduced herself, as well as her daughter, Georgiana Cutter, and Georgiana's sister-in-law, Dana. Laura noticed Georgiana holding Dana's forearm, and it didn't take but a moment for her to realize the pretty strawberry-haired woman was blind.

"We got the book on CD for Georgiana," Dana explained as they sat down.

"Yes, and I'm so glad we did," Georgiana said. "Tamar's story touched my heart."

"Mine, too," Laura admitted, taking her seat in the center chair and preparing to lead the discussion. "I started reading it Sunday afternoon and couldn't go to sleep that night until I was done, well after two o'clock."

Mandy sat next to Laura. They'd grown very close over the past few weeks, with Laura visiting Mandy nearly every day at the photography studio. She leaned toward Laura and said softly, "I really wanted you to read that story."

"I appreciate that," Laura said, "more than you could know."

She'd never read the story of Tamar, either, and she had no idea how terribly the lady had been treated by the men she tried to love. Nor did she know about the way Tamar had tricked her father-in-law into fathering her child. But in spite of her trickery, God favored her for attaining her natural rights when she'd been wronged by Judah's sons. And she ended up being one of only five women listed in the lineage of Christ.

Laura cleared her throat. "So, we have some discussion questions here. I'd like to get your thoughts on these. Question one, Tamar was abused, abandoned and neglected. She ended up taking matters into her own hands and having a difficult time of it. Have you ever felt like this?"

To Laura's relief, the women in the group were very open, with several of them bringing up instances in their lives where they'd experienced a hard time, often because they were trying to handle things on their own. Jessica spoke up first and talked about her fear when she'd become pregnant as a teen and how she'd hidden the pregnancy from Chad so he wouldn't give up his college scholarship.

"If I'd have told him the truth and hadn't run away, we'd have had six more years together raising Nathan. But I thought I'd messed up, and I didn't want to mess up his life, too." She brushed a tear away then added, "But Nathan completes his life, completes our lives. He and Lainey are the best parts of our world."

"I tried running away from God," Mandy said softly, "after Mia died. I know now that I was blaming Him. But He wanted me back—" she pointed to the book in her hand "—the same way He wanted Tamar."

"Enough to put her in the lineage of His Son," Mary said. "I think that's a beautiful image of how very much He wants us, don't you? Even when we feel we've messed up?"

All of the women agreed, and Laura swallowed thickly through the lump in her throat. She'd come to the same realization reading Tamar's story, but to hear her thoughts voiced by all of the other women, and to learn that they'd had moments where they felt like they'd turned their backs on God, too...overwhelmed her.

She glanced up and saw David leaning against one of the endcaps looking toward the group but undeniably focused on her. He tilted his head, held up the okay symbol with his hand and mouthed, You okay?

Laura's heart was filled with compassion toward Mandy, for convincing her to read this story, and toward David, for seeing her through the past few weeks and encouraging her to come back to God without shoving her through the church door. Very okay, she mouthed.

He smiled then turned and went to the counter apparently convinced that she would be fine. And, through question after question and discussion after discussion, she was. In fact, she was more than fine. For the first time in as long as she could remember, Laura felt...blessed.

Chapter Eleven

Laura checked the clock in her bedroom—11:45 a.m. David and his parents would be here any minute to pick her up to go to the church Thanksgiving dinner, and she couldn't decide what to wear. Four complete outfits were strewn haphazardly across the bed, and none of them had seemed right for meeting David's parents.

It wasn't as if she hadn't met them before. She'd met them plenty of times at UT when they visited David on campus; however, she'd never been nearly eight months pregnant with twins when she saw them. And she'd never really been trying to make an impression. But today, she was.

Last night, she'd attended the midweek Bible study with David at the church, and like Mandy had promised, everyone welcomed her with open arms. She'd felt accepted, forgiven, loved. David never left her side and introduced her to anyone she hadn't already met. Laura had enjoyed Brother Henry's class about grace and felt right at home in the small community church. In fact, she wondered why she'd stayed away from church, away from God, so long. And she wondered why she'd never realized how amazing David was when they were in school. He'd always been a dear friend, but she'd never thought of him beyond that. Now, as much as she'd fought it, she couldn't *stop* thinking about him that way, and she wondered if they'd ever have a real date.

Then again, she shouldn't have to wonder. He said if it happened, she'd know. Would it ever happen?

She heard the door downstairs and then a female voice calling, "Laura?"

"Oh, dear." Taking a look in the mirror, she saw that she'd ended up in a long stretchy navy dress. She'd yet to accessorize, and she had no idea about shoes.

"Laura, you here, dear?"

David's mother. Laura couldn't start their day together by keeping her waiting, so she headed down the stairs.

"I'm so sorry. I'm running behind," she said, entering the kitchen to find Mrs. Presley waving her hand through the smoke and attempting to turn down the knob on the oven. "Oh, no, I forgot all about the pie!" Laura hurried to help the lady as she opened the oven door, and more smoke came rolling out to fill the kitchen. And then, naturally, the smoke detector emitted a deafening screech.

"Where are your pot holders?" Mrs. Presley asked, all calm and cool in spite of the incessant blast, which seemed to be getting louder.

Laura coughed. "Over there, on the counter by the refrigerator."

David and his father entered the smoky room and quickly evaluated the situation. "Laura, Mom, y'all get out of this smoke," David said. "Dad, can you—"

"Open the doors and windows?" his father asked. "One step ahead of you." He'd already flung the back door open, and he unlocked a window and pushed it up, then moved to the next and did the same.

Thankfully, the smoke thinned out fairly quickly, and nothing was actually flaming.

"I'm so sorry," Laura said. "I wanted to make a pie for the lunch and then I was having a hard time picking out what to wear, and I forgot all about it."

David waved a hand above the charred meringue. "Well, it looks like it would have been—" he hesitated "—real good. What was it, chocolate?"

"Lemon," Laura said miserably. "Lemon icebox."

David's father was the first one to smother his laugh, but David couldn't hold his back, and it rolled out with gusto. His mother's lips were pressed together as though she were afraid to open them or she'd also set a laugh free.

Laura frowned. "I was just going to brown the meringue for a second."

"Well, it *is* brown," David said, pointing to the blackened mound of what used to be fluffy white topping. Then he laughed again, and this time, Laura joined in.

Apparently, Mrs. Presley was simply waiting for Laura's cue, because she released a giggle that Laura was pretty certain had a bit of a snort in the middle.

When they finally finished laughing and the room cleared of most of the smoke, David glanced at Laura's feet, sticking out beneath the dress. "Laura, were you planning to go without shoes?"

"No," she said. "I couldn't decide on what to wear, and I was in the middle of considering this dress when your mom came in and then I remembered the pie. Or rather, I never remembered it, I smelled it."

David's mother wrapped an arm around her and started toward the stairs. "Tell you what. You guys finish cleaning up and airing this place out down here. I'll help Laura get ready. Sound good?"

David and his father nodded in unison, and Laura let the lady guide her to her room.

"You'll have to forgive the mess," she said. "I was having a tough time deciding."

"This isn't a mess," Mrs. Presley said as she looked at the discarded clothes, "it's the sign of a woman getting ready."

"Thanks. I'm so sorry that we're going to be late. I'll hurry and pick something out."

"I like the dress you have on," she said.

"You do?" Laura ran a hand along the jersey fabric. "I did, too, to tell you the truth, but I wasn't sure what to put with it."

"How about this?" She picked the gold cardigan from Laura's closet. "And you have these matching flats. How about a chunky bracelet to go with it, maybe a red one?"

Laura moved to her jewelry box and withdrew a red cuff bracelet. "Like this one?"

"Perfect," she said, smiling as Laura snapped the bracelet in place. "And you know, I have a beautiful new red infinity scarf in the car. We'll add that when we go outside, and I think that'll tie it all together very nicely."

Laura was amazed. Her mother often coordinated clothes and usually gave Laura complete ensembles so that she never had to worry about mixing and matching items on her own. But watching Mrs. Presley in action was fun. "You're very good at that," she said.

David's mother spotted some gold earrings on the dresser and handed them to Laura. She tilted her head as Laura put the earrings on and then nodded her approval. "I've never had a daughter to shop with or to help dress. This is fun." She looked at Laura and didn't hide the fact that she noticed her tummy.

"Mrs. Presley," Laura began, feeling that she should explain.

David's mother spoke before Laura had a chance. "We're very happy for you," she said tenderly, "and your babies. Children are a gift from God, you know."

Laura's heart tugged in her chest. "I know."

"And we're glad you came to David. He told us about you working at the store and how you've boosted his business. I'll be honest, we've been worried that the bookstore wasn't going to make it, not because of anything he's said, but because it didn't seem to have a lot happening anytime we would visit. It's good to see that it's working again. And I'm grateful to you for helping that happen."

"I enjoy working there," Laura said. "And I'm very grateful for all of David's help. I, well, I don't know what I'd have done—or what I'd do—without him." She hadn't meant to say so much, but it was hard to talk about David now without attempting to explain how much he was beginning to mean to her, almost even more because she hadn't wanted to feel anything toward her boss, toward her friend. But she was definitely starting to feel something.

His mother ran a finger along her cheek and smiled. "You're helping him, too, dear. And in case you've wondered about it, I don't want you to have any misconceptions. David's father and I are very happy about that. Whatever happens between you and our son, we *are* happy about it." Her smile ease up a notch. "You understand?"

Laura did understand, and the realization tha David's mother had essentially said that she wa happy about a relationship between Laura and he son both shocked and thrilled her. "I do understand and thank you."

"No, thank you. We haven't seen him this happ in a very long time," she said, "and from what h says, you haven't even been on a real date."

Laura couldn't control her surprise. "He told yo that?"

"Not voluntarily, but as a mother, I've learne what questions to ask. I bet you'll figure out ho to do the same with your girls."

Laura thought about the future conversation she'd have with her daughters. "I'm sure I will. They left the bedroom and found the two men wait ing at the bottom of the stairs.

"I get it," David said. "I told you I couldn't cook and you were trying to make me feel better."

"Very funny." Laura tried to stomp past him, bu he tossed an arm around her and pulled her close.

"It was sweet of you to want to fix a pie, but the will have plenty of food. I bet they won't even mis it," he said as they passed through the semi-smok kitchen and walked outside. "But I bet you'll mak some stray cat's day." He pointed to the garbage ca behind the studio and the charred pie balanced on top of the bags.

Laura laughed, with David and his parents joining in, and then they drove to the church and she had her best Thanksgiving dinner ever.

The next morning, the bookstore opened at 8:00 a.m. to join in the Black Friday "Sales on the Square." Laura's father called shortly after and said he was on his way, and she looked forward to him arriving and being part of today's fun. Customers filled the store and were steadily purchasing all of the inspirational gift books Laura had recommended David order for the holidays, as well as many other books in the store.

"The Christmas favorites display is a hit," David said, placing a large stuffed snowman in the chair beside the display. "I've always advertised the classics at Christmas, but you were right—putting the modern stories here as well has really been popular."

"Adults love the classics, but the teens are typically looking for something a little more trendy," his mother said. "Laura got it right."

"Thanks." Laura helped another customer looking for Destiny's book. "And it looks like *Southern Love in Claremont* is going to be a popular stocking stuffer this year."

"That'll make Destiny happy," David said.

Mr. Presley stayed behind the counter ringing up

and visiting with customers while Laura, David and Mrs. Presley replenished the items on the displays and helped customers find their desired books. It didn't seem like four hours had passed when Laura's dad walked in.

She didn't realize how much she'd missed him until she saw him enter the store. "Daddy!" Laura hurried to him and hugged him tightly.

He kissed her cheek. "Hey, princess. How's it going?"

"It was going good, but now that you're here it's going great!" she said.

"Now that's a smile I've missed seeing," he said. "I can't wait to tell your mom how good you're doing."

Laura was often mesmerized by her father's love toward her mom. Obviously, Marjorie Holland wasn't easy to love, but that never stopped either of them from loving her just the same. "Mom called me this morning," Laura said. "Just to let me know she was sorry she couldn't come with you and that she'd call me again tonight after she got done at work."

He nodded. "I wish she could've come, too."

"Mr. Holland," David said. It took him a moment to maneuver past the children crowding around the boxcar to get to Laura's dad. He extended a hand. "We're glad you're here."

"Thanks, David. I'm glad to be here, especially

because I get to see my Laura smiling again," he said. "Thank you for that."

"Happy to help." David winked at Laura then glanced down to see the child tugging at his arm.

"Hey, Mr. David, can you come help us?"

Laura recognized the boy as Matthew Hayes, one of the twins. "Matthew, is there something I can help you with?" she asked.

"Nah, I just threw one of the pillows up high and it got stuck on the top shelf. Can you get it down, Mr. David, like, before Daddy sees it?"

David laughed. "Duty calls," he said, following Matthew to the scene of the crime. "I'll be right back."

"I like that young man," her father said as they watched David retrieve the pillow and then hand it back to the kids.

"I do, too." And that had become a major understatement over the past few days.

Laura watched as David made certain the kids knew the pillows should stay at ground level then returned smiling. "Hey, since my folks are here to help me out in the store, why don't you go show your dad around the square? Take some time to visit, and go have lunch or something."

Laura did want to spend some time alone with her dad, but she didn't want to abandon David on the busy sale day. "You sure?"

"Of course. Besides, my dad and I need to run

to the building supply store later for a project I've got going upstairs, so we'll trade. You and your dad can help my mom out here when we leave, and we'll call it even."

"When does your mom get a break?" Laura asked.

"Are you kidding? She's on cloud nine around all of these kids." He pointed to Mrs. Presley, sitting in the children's area and animatedly reading to the kids, who were captivated with her rendition of *Frosty the Snowman*. "I'll be lucky if I can talk her into retreating to the kitchen long enough to eat a sandwich."

Laura had to agree. David's mom appeared to be having a blast. "Okay, then, we'll head out and then tag team with you and your dad in an hour or so."

"Make it two hours. It's going to be a long day, and you'll want that extra break," he said. Then to Laura's dad, he said, "Don't let her overdo it on the walking. I try to watch and make sure she sits down and rests often, but she doesn't always listen."

"Sounds like he's got you pegged." Her dad wrapped an arm around her and then looked back to David. "Don't worry, we won't overdo it."

Laura liked the fact that both of them wanted to take care of her. "Thanks, but I will stop if I get tired."

"And we'll make sure you keep that promise," her father said.

Laura didn't argue. There had been a couple of

afternoons that David practically had to force her to take a break. She'd wanted everything perfect for the sale today and hadn't wanted to waste any time. But they were right. She was at the point in the pregnancy where she had to be careful and not overexert. Early labor was always a possibility with twins.

"So, you ready?" her dad asked.

"I am." She led him out of the bookstore and into the square. People filled the sidewalk, and signage advertising each merchant's Black Friday sales covered the storefronts. "What do you think?" she asked.

"I think your mother should've come," he said. "She would've loved all of this. Marjorie has spent so many Black Fridays at Macy's that she doesn't even realize there are more activities going on, like this type of old-fashioned thing. Look at that fountain and the geese. And all of these detailed storefronts. The architecture is remarkable. It's like someone plucked the entire town out of the fifties."

"I know. I love it here," she admitted.

"I'm glad for that. I really am. I meant what I told David. It's wonderful to see you smile again."

"I've been smiling a lot lately," she said, saying hello to several shoppers that she recognized from the bookstore and church as they walked down the sidewalk. Everyone was so friendly, and she realized that she already felt at home in Claremont. "So for lunch, how about one of the best cheeseburgers you'll ever taste?" She pointed across the square. "You're going to love Nelson's."

"Lead the way." He walked beside her, and when they reached the variety store, Marvin Tolleson met them at the door.

"Miss Laura, great to see you!" he said. "I've had several customers come in with bags from the bookstore. Looks like y'all are having a good day."

"We are." She nodded toward the packed booths and soda fountain. "And it looks like you are, too."

"God is blessing us," he agreed, "but don't worry. We have an open booth in the back for you. And I don't believe we've met." He smiled at Laura's father.

"Thomas Holland. I'm Laura's dad."

"Well, then, I believe I met your wife here a few weeks back," Marvin said, ushering them toward the only vacant booth. "Nice lady, but I'll admit, I thought she was Miss Laura's sister when she first came in."

Her father grinned. "We get that a lot, but I take it as a compliment, as does she."

"Well, here are your menus." He handed them each a laminated sheet. "Do you know what you want to drink?"

"I'll have sweet tea," her dad said.

"I'll have the large lemonade," Laura said, "and we can go ahead and order, if that's okay."

"The babies hungry?" her father asked.

Laura grinned. "Always."

"Well, we can take care of that," Marvin said. "What would you like?"

"Cheeseburger and sweet potato fries." It'd become one of her favorite meals.

"I'll have the same," her dad said as his phone started up with the "Rocky Top" ring tone. He withdrew it from his pocket and glanced at the display. Laura knew before he answered that it was her mom.

"Hey, how's work going?" He nodded a few times as she apparently told him about her morning, or night would be more accurate, since the sale started at midnight. "I'm sitting at a table with her right now for lunch. Yes, it is really nice here."

He continued talking for a few minutes and then said, "You get yourself something to eat while you have a chance. I'm glad you're having a good sales day." Another nod. "I'll tell her." He smiled. "I love you, too. 'Bye." He pocketed the phone. "She wanted me to tell you she loves you and misses you, and that she'll be back down here soon."

"I'd like that," Laura said as Marvin's wife, Mae, hurried toward the table with two plates of food.

"Marvin said your babies are hungry—" she placed a plate in front of each of them "—so we moved your order to the top."

Laura laughed. "I could've waited." She plucked a fry from the plate and started eating it.

"But we didn't want you to," Mae said. "And

Marvin told me you're Laura's dad. We're glad you're here."

"Glad to be here," he said.

They started eating, but Laura didn't have her food on her mind. True, she was hungry, and she'd eat, but she also wanted to talk about what had been bothering her ever since her mother's visit. "Dad, when Mom came down, she seemed to really enjoy herself and we had a great day," she said.

"That's what she said. I wished she'd have told me she was coming down here, but I am glad you two enjoyed some time together."

"Me, too, but—" she decided just to tell him what happened "—but before she left, she said some things that confused me."

He was about to take another bite of cheeseburger, but he placed the sandwich back on his plate. "Something about why she keeps leaving? Because I asked her, again, and I got the same answer."

"What answer?"

"That she had to get away." He shrugged. "Same answer she's been giving me for nearly twenty-four years. Did she tell you something different?"

The eagerness in his tone hurt Laura. He so wanted to know what caused his wife to head out every now and then, and Laura wanted to know, too. Over the past few weeks, ever since she spent that day with her mom, she'd thought about the best words to convey everything her mother said, and she selected them carefully now. "She started off talking about you, the two of you, and how you were the love of her life, and that she thought she fell in love with you the first time she saw you."

His mouth flattened, and he nodded. "She's told me that before, and I believe her. I felt the same way. There's something to be said for love at first sight."

Laura imagined her parents young and so in love, and she liked the image. She almost didn't want to tell him the rest, but she knew how desperately he wanted to figure out what caused her mother to run. "But then she said something else through the day that I couldn't stop thinking about, something I didn't understand."

"What'd she say?" He'd pushed his plate forward, having lost all interest in eating until he and Laura had this conversation.

"She said that she wanted me to find someone who chose *me*. A couple of times she mentioned how important it was to be with someone who chose you." Laura shook her head, not understanding it any more now than she did that day. "Is there something that has happened in your marriage to make her think she wasn't your first choice? Or when you were dating?" Laura asked. "That's all I can think of."

He sat there for a second then ran his hand down his face while Laura took in his instant reaction. Maybe he did know what was going on with her mom.

"Daddy?" she asked while he straightened in the booth then leaned his head back against the seat and whispered something to the ceiling.

Laura couldn't hear his words for all of the chatter in the five-and-dime, but she read his lips.

"Oh, Marjorie, what do I have to do to make you believe me?"

Laura leaned forward in her seat and lowered her voice, though that hardly mattered with the crowd and the noise today. Even so, she didn't want to draw undue attention to whatever her father was about to say. "Daddy, did you—was there someone else that you loved?"

He slid his hand across the table, took Laura's in his and squeezed. "Honey, there has never been anyone else. Like I said earlier, I think I fell in love with your mom the first time I saw her."

"Then what is she talking about, wanting to be the one someone chooses? Why doesn't she feel like you chose her?" Laura was so thankful for Marvin's crowd now. Normally, it'd be impossible to have this conversation at the restaurant, but thanks to the Black Friday shoppers, that wasn't a problem. And Laura was glad; she didn't want to wait to hear his answer.

"She isn't talking about another woman," he said. "She's talking about...you."

Chapter Twelve

"Me?" Laura didn't see that coming. Her mother had never seemed jealous of her relationship with her father; she was certain of it. They were all close in spite of her mother's quirks. But surely if her mom didn't like the fact that Laura and her dad were close, Laura would have been able to tell, right? "What do you mean…me?"

He took a deep breath, let it out. Then he glanced at the surrounding tables to apparently make sure no one was listening to their conversation.

No one was. Everyone was busily chatting and eating and absorbed in discussing the activities of the day.

"Daddy, tell me what you're talking about."

He nodded. "Honey, you know that your mom was several months pregnant when we married."

Laura, of course, knew. Her parents were married in August, and Laura was born in February.

It hadn't been a secret. She nodded and waited for him to continue.

"Back then, when she told me, and I said we'd get married, she said she didn't want me to marry her just because she was pregnant."

The pieces clicked into place, and Laura suddenly felt sorry for her mom. "She didn't think you would have married her if she hadn't been pregnant." Laura knew times had changed over the years. Back then, when a girl was pregnant, the couple typically married. Nowadays, for example with Jared, marrying Laura hadn't even occurred to him; he'd merely wanted her to end the pregnancy.

"I told her then that I had already known I wanted to marry her. Sure, it was quicker than we planned. She was only seventeen, and I was eighteen. But we would have married anyway. I'm sure of it, and I told her so. I thought she believed me." He shook his head. "All of these years, *that* was why she kept running away?"

Laura remembered more of what her mother said during her visit. "She said that everything had been harder this year, because of me and Jared. I didn't understand what she meant, but now I do. Me getting pregnant, and then Jared not even considering marriage to me—even marrying someone else—probably made her wonder if that's what you wanted back then."

"But it isn't, Laura. I always wanted your mother.

I've always loved her, and I always will." He exhaled thickly. "I just don't know what I have to do to prove it to her."

Laura had pushed her plate to the center of the table, but she pulled it back and picked up a fry. She felt better, somehow, at least knowing what was going on in her mother's mind. And she was determined to help her father show his wife that he'd always chosen *her*. Pointing the fry at her dad, she said, "Well, then, that's our goal today, to figure out how you can prove it."

He'd looked miserable a moment ago, but his eyes lit up, and one corner of his mouth lifted as he also reached for his discarded plate. "You have any ideas?"

She ate another fry then picked up her burger. "Not yet, but I'm not letting you leave here today until we figure something out."

He laughed. "Your determination. You get that from her, you know."

Laura smiled. "I know."

"And your good looks from me," he said with a wink, which caused both of them to laugh. Laura was the spitting image of her mother, and her father would be the first one to say so.

"I love you, Daddy," she said, then continued working on her cheeseburger.

"Love you right back," he said, then did the same.

They talked about things that might let Marjorie see how much he cared.

"How about a nice vacation, something like a second honeymoon?" Laura asked.

"That's what the cruise was supposed to be, and obviously that didn't do the trick."

"Jewelry?"

"I gave her a new necklace for her birthday, and she liked it, but no, I don't think that's the answer. She usually buys jewelry to match the clothes she gets at the store, so that isn't typically something she wants."

"Flowers," Laura said. She couldn't ever remember her father sending her mother flowers.

He shook his head. "Your mother never has liked flowers. She said they just die and remind her of funerals."

Laura squished her nose at that. "Gee, thanks for ruining the way I think of them, Mom."

He grinned at that. "There's got to be something I can do."

Laura pondered it while she ate but wasn't coming up with anything. She was still thinking about it when a cute Asian girl bounced up to the booth. Laura had noticed her moving around the restaurant from table to table, but she'd been too absorbed in her thoughts about her mother to pay much attention. The girl was a teen, sixteen or seventeen, Laura would guess.

"Hi," she said, "do you have any Secret Santa stories you'd like to share for the *Claremont News*?" Then she looked up from her small notepad and said, "Oh, hey, you're not from Claremont, are you?"

"I'm not," Laura's father said, "but my daughter moved here a few weeks ago." He pointed to Laura.

"Oh, yeah, I met you Wednesday night at church," she said. "I'm Nadia Berry. Brother Henry is my grandfather."

Laura nodded, the memory clicking into place. "I remember now." Then she asked, "You said something about a Secret Santa?"

"Oh, yes," Nadia said. "See, I'm hoping to get a degree in journalism after high school. I'm a senior now. And the newspaper is letting me intern there. They're letting me do a seasonal story on Claremont's Secret Santa. Have you not heard about our Secret Santa yet?"

Laura shook her head.

"Oh, well, it's pretty awesome," Nadia said. "See, several years ago—we can't figure out exactly when it started, which is something I'm trying to determine for my article—a Secret Santa started helping folks out in Claremont at Christmastime. Usually, the things start happening the day after Thanksgiving, which is today, and that's why I wanted to write a story about it."

"What kind of things?" Laura's father asked.

"Clothes for kids that need them, groceries and

things like that. But also bigger things," she said, glancing at her notepad. "One man said that he couldn't make his mortgage one Christmas and didn't know how his kids were even going to have a Christmas, and Secret Santa paid his note and delivered toys for the kids. Another lady said she had hospital bills that she couldn't pay, and when she called in December to get the balance, she learned it'd been paid by Secret Santa. He's known to do big things like that, but also little things, like leaving candy canes for people to find and so they'll see where he's been. But I'm pretty sure lots of folks put the candy canes out now, just because it's fun and to throw people off his trail." Nadia grinned. "See, we really don't want to know who it is. We just like talking about it. It's fun for it to be a mystery, don't you think?"

"Yes, I do," Laura said, amazed at all of the uniqueness of this small Alabama town. A Secret Santa.

"Everyone loves surprises," Nadia continued, "especially when it means something special or helps you out in a big way." She looked at her notes. "It's like Mandy Brantley said earlier, 'It doesn't have to be anything huge, just something to let a person know someone cares and understands how they feel.'" Nadia looked up from the pad. "Mandy said Secret Santa sent her a card the first Christmas after she lost Mia and also sent a Bible storybook for

Kaden that became his favorite. It was the story of Moses," Nadia said. "I'm definitely going to include that in my article."

"Well, I don't have a Secret Santa story to share since I just moved here," Laura said, "but I look forward to your article. It sounds like you're going to do a great job."

"Thanks!" Nadia exclaimed, and then said to Laura's father, "Nice to meet you."

"You, too," he said, finishing off his fries and smiling.

"What is it?" Laura asked.

"I think I have an idea for what I should do for your mom."

Ten minutes later they were back on the square. "What's your idea?" she asked.

"I thought I spotted…" He scanned the storefronts. "Yep, there it is. I knew I saw one. Come on." He walked purposefully, but Laura had no clue where they were headed.

"Where are we going?"

"You'll see."

She spotted the Tiny Tots Treasure Box toy store, Gina Brown's Art Gallery, The Grind coffee shop and The Sweet Stop candy shop in their path. But she didn't think any of those would have something that he'd want to buy her mother.

Then he stopped in front of the Claremont Jewelry Store and gazed at a collection of rings in the window.

"I thought you said she didn't like jewelry," Laura said as he moved toward the door and walked in.

"She doesn't like any ol' jewelry," he said. "But everyone likes surprises, especially when they mean something special," he added, quoting Nadia.

Laura wasn't sure what he had in mind, but she followed him over to the ring cases. There was only one gentleman working at the store. Laura remembered meeting him at church Wednesday night and again yesterday at the Thanksgiving dinner but couldn't recall his name. He finished up with another customer, then moved to the opposite side of the jewelry case from Laura and her dad.

"Well, hello. It's Laura, isn't it?" he said. His voice was so kind and friendly, and again Laura struggled to remember the name.

"I'm so sorry," she said. "I met so many people at church…."

"No problem," he said with a smile, "there are a lot of people to meet in Claremont. A lot of folks have told me about what a good job you're doing at the bookstore. My grandson comes to the book club with you on Mondays, and he's loving it." Then he shook his head and added, "I'm Marvin, by the way. Marvin Grier. And I own the jewelry store here. Is there anything I can help you with?"

"Wedding rings," her father said.

"Okay. Are we looking for an anniversary type band or a traditional set?"

"Traditional set."

Laura watched in amazement as Mr. Grier withdrew two satin-lined trays of stunning wedding rings. The bell on the door sounded as another customer came in behind them, and Mr. Grier said, "I'm going to help him and give you a little privacy while you make your decision. Just let me know if you have any questions."

"We will," Thomas said. He waited for Mr. Grier to move farther away and then explained, "When we first got married, I didn't have any money to pay for a nice ring. I asked her on our ten-year and then our twenty-year anniversary if she wanted a nicer one, but she said she didn't, that she loved the one I gave her in the beginning."

"I'm sure she does," Laura said.

"But our wedding was so quiet and low-key, and so was our engagement. We just wanted to get everything done quickly and be married. It didn't really give her the chance to enjoy the moment, you know." He frowned. "I asked her to marry me, but there was no surprise to it. She went with me to pick out the ring, and then we put it on her hand right there in the store. And then we went to the courthouse and got married."

Laura had never really thought about the details of her parents' wedding before, and now it seemed like it wasn't all that special.

"I want to give her a ring that tells her if I had a

chance to do it all again, I'd choose her, and I'd give her a ring like this." He picked up a huge marquise solitaire. "She always liked this cut." He handed it to Laura. "Try it on for me, will you? Y'all wear the same size ring, don't you?"

"Yes," Laura said, and before she could stop him, he slid the ring on her finger. She stared at the sparkling huge stone. "Wow, Daddy. That's really something."

"You think she'll like it?"

"It looks like Mom," Laura admitted, taking another glance and then sliding the ring from her finger.

"I think so, too." He held it up to the light and admired the way it shone. Then he checked the price tag and winced.

"You don't have to get something so big," Laura said, knowing he didn't make a lot of money and probably didn't have that kind of cash lying around to purchase an extravagant ring.

"Yeah, I do," he said, "and I've been tucking away money into savings over the years. I can't think of any better reason to spend some of it." He grinned. "I'm going to do it right this time, down on one knee, the whole nine yards. And I'm going to make sure Marjorie knows that I chose her then, and I'd choose her all over again. Thinking I'll give it to her on Christmas, so keep it a secret, okay?"

"Okay." Laura nodded. "That's a wonderful idea, Daddy."

Thomas kept looking at the ring he'd selected, while Laura's attention focused on another set. The ring had two small stones on either side of one a little larger, nowhere near as big as the one her father had selected, but in Laura's opinion, quite elegant. Beautiful.

"You want to try that one on?" Mr. Grier asked, and Laura realized that she'd been so enthralled with the pretty ring that she hadn't heard him return.

"Oh, no, I don't have any reason to," she said, but her father and Mr. Grier urged her.

"Try it on," her dad said, and Mr. Grier lifted the ring and slid it on her finger.

"A perfect fit, don't you think?" he said as the bell on the door sounded and another customer must have entered. Laura didn't turn to verify the fact, her attention unable to veer from the sight of that ring. She'd never had a wedding ring on her finger before, but she couldn't deny it looked good there. Felt good there, too.

"That's right pretty on you, Miss Laura."

She turned to see Zeb Shackleford standing behind her and peering at the ring.

"Oh, I was just, I don't know, trying one on since my dad is looking at one for my mom," she stammered. "Mr. Zeb, this is my dad, Thomas Shackelford." She shook her head. "Thomas Holland, I mean. Sorry."

"Nice to meet you," Zeb said.

"You, too," her father answered, then turned his attention to Mr. Grier to discuss payment options.

Laura slipped the ring off and fumbled to put it back in the tray. "Don't know what I was thinking," she said, attempting a laugh toward Zeb.

The older man simply nodded as though he knew exactly what she was thinking, dreaming.

While her father continued surveying the ring in the light and attempting to make his final decision, Mr. Grier touched the one Laura had tried on. "Those are princess-cut diamonds," he said. "The three stones represent the past, present and future trio of your love."

As if the ring wasn't already calling Laura's name, she was even more drawn to it because of the symbolization. "That's beautiful," she said, then she turned her attention back to the person actually planning to purchase a ring today. "So, Daddy, what did you decide?"

"I'll take it," he said.

"That's great," Mr. Grier answered, and then they walked toward the back of the store to let Laura's father pay for his purchase.

"No harm in trying on wedding rings and dreaming a bit," Zeb said softly.

"I suppose not," she said, sneaking another peek

at the ring before looking into Zeb's kind face. "What are you shopping for, Mr. Zeb?" He mentioned nearly every day that his sweet Dolly had passed on and that he looked forward to seeing her again. He also mentioned that they hadn't had any children, which was why he was so attached to all of the kids he read to each week. So Laura wondered who he was buying jewelry for.

"One of the girls at the hospital, her name is Faith," he said. "She has a charm bracelet and wanted some new charms for Christmas. I asked Mr. Grier to order one that I thought she'd like."

Mr. Grier had apparently finished taking her father's payment because the two of them made their way back to where Zeb and Laura stood by the display case.

"Zeb, your charm came in yesterday," Mr. Grier said, reaching beneath the counter and pulling out a small white box.

"You want to see it?" Zeb asked Laura.

"Sure."

Mr. Grier opened the box to reveal a tiny pink heart charm.

Zeb's mouth rolled in as he looked at the tiny charm. "We call Faith a little sweetheart," he said. "She wasn't supposed to make it this long, but God had other plans. She's still hanging on and touches all of our hearts every time we see her." He touched the delicate heart. "And her favorite color is pink. So I thought this was perfect."

Laura was moved by the elderly man's thoughtfulness. "It's incredible," she said. "David and I are still going with you next week to read to the children at the hospital, right?"

"I'd hoped you would. I'd like for you to meet them, and for them to meet you."

"I'm looking forward to meeting Faith," she said.

"I'm looking forward to you meeting her, too. Faith, well, Faith will change your life."

Chapter Thirteen

Whimsical murals from stories in the Bible covered the walls of the children's floor at Claremont Hospital. Zeb led Laura and David past the floor's lobby, which displayed a huge Noah's Ark scene, complete with fun, colorful animals lining up in pairs to hop on the boat. In the distance, a bright rainbow filled the sky, and the words *I have set my rainbow in the clouds* hovered in the center.

"That's gorgeous," Laura said.

"Why, thanks." A nurse wearing scrubs covered in teddy bears stepped away from the nurse's station to greet them. Her name tag read Shea Farmer. "We got the murals two years ago. As a matter of fact, they'll be mentioned in the paper this week in an article Nadia Berry is working on about Secret Santa."

"Secret Santa painted your murals?" David asked. "Didn't you kind of figure out who it was when you saw them painting?"

The lady laughed. "No, Secret Santa didn't paint them, but he sent the money to a woman who did the work. And it was pretty awesome, because she had been several months without employment, and she said the money she received for the murals helped her catch up on her bills and also allowed her family to have a real Christmas."

"That's wonderful," Laura said.

"I know," she said. "So, Zeb, the kids have been especially looking forward to tonight's visit, since you told them you were bringing some friends."

"Are they all in the playroom, Shea?" Zeb asked.

"Everyone except Faith," she said. "I told her you'd visit her room."

Laura recognized the name from the jewelry store. The little girl for whom Zeb bought the charm and whose favorite color was pink.

"She had a rough day?" Zeb asked.

"The day after chemo is always rough," Shea said, "but I know it'll cheer her up to see you."

Zeb nodded and then continued down the hall to a large room with toys and books bordering the walls and a group of children seated in the center.

"Hey, Mr. Zeb!" a little boy called. He looked about the same age as Kaden, but his skin didn't have the rosy glow that Kaden's had. Instead it was pale, if not tinged slightly yellow. "Are those your friends?"

"Yes, Avery, this is Mr. David and Miss Laura,

who I told you about. Mr. David owns the bookstore that gives y'all the books we read."

"Cool!" another boy said. He sat in a wheelchair with a portable IV hooked up to a rolling pole. He had red hair and freckles and a beautiful smile.

"What's your name?" Laura asked.

"I'm Timothy, but you can call me Timmy if you want. That's what everyone else does. I'm seven."

"Well it's nice to meet you, Timmy," she said.

Zeb addressed the kids. "Now, like I told you last week, Mr. David and Miss Laura are going to start coming with me sometimes and will be reading to you from the *Boxcar Children* books. They've been reading them with some other kids at their bookstore each week and thought you might enjoy them, too."

Laura held up her copy of the book. "Ready to get started?"

They all nodded or answered "Yes!" and Laura took a seat in the middle of the group then opened the book to the first page.

"If it's okay with all of you," Zeb said, "Mr. David and I are going to walk down the hall and visit Faith while Miss Laura reads."

A little girl with brown pigtails bobbed her head. "Faith will like that," she said.

"That good for you?" David asked Laura.

She nodded. "Yes, it's fine." More than fine, really, because these children were undeniably anxious to hear the story, and she realized as she read that they were even happier about sharing the story than the kids in her weekly book club. The boys and girls surrounding her were confined to a hospital room the majority of their day. But now, as they leaned forward to hear every word about the story, they escaped their sickness, escaped their pain and lost themselves in the world of the *Boxcar Children*.

Laura read for an hour, answering questions whenever any child raised their hand, and she loved every minute. When Shea reappeared, Laura was saddened that it was time to leave, but the nurse explained amid the children's groans of disappointment that it was time for them to go to bed.

"I'll come back tomorrow if you like," Laura said.

They all clapped, and she smiled, happy to have this opportunity and grateful to Zeb for giving it to her. "Where is Faith's room, Shea?"

The nurse had started wheeling Timothy out, and the little boy answered, "She's at two twenty-four," he said, still smiling. He hadn't stopped smiling for the past hour.

"Thank you, Timmy," Laura said, then headed toward the room.

She found David and Zeb sitting on each side of the bed holding cards. The little girl, wearing a sequined pink cap to cover her lack of hair, plucked a card from David's hand.

"Another match for me," she said, then noticed Laura. "Hey, are you Miss Laura?"

Laura neared the bed. "I am."

"Mr. Zeb said you'll read to me next time and catch me up on what I missed with the *Boxcar Children*."

"I'd love to," Laura said. "I think I'm coming back tomorrow night. Maybe I can come in here first and read to you before I read to the others."

Faith's smile beamed. "That sounds great!" She watched as David grabbed a card from Zeb's hand, and then giggled when Zeb had to take one from hers. "I've only got two left," she said, "and guess what one of them is."

Zeb held his finger in front of one, tilted his head as he watched her eyes, blinking mischievously, and then took the other card.

Faith's giggle filled the room. "Old maid for you," she said.

Laura watched them continue until, sure enough, Zeb's last card was the unwanted lady.

"You lose again, Mr. Zeb," Faith said.

"And so I do," he said.

A young woman who looked to be in her early thirties walked in, her eyes bloodshot and undeniably tired, but she gave them all a smile. "Did you let Zeb win tonight, honey?"

"Nope," Faith said.

"I wouldn't know what to do if I won," Zeb answered, and Faith grinned.

"Thank you for playing with me," she said, "and you, too, Mr. David."

"It was my pleasure," David said.

"And you must be Laura," the woman said. "I'm Sharon Mulberry, Faith's mom."

"Wonderful to meet you," Laura said.

Faith stretched her jaw wide in a huge yawn, and her mother stepped forward to gather the cards from the bed.

"I think that's your clue that you need to sleep now," she said.

"I know. Thanks again for coming, Mr. Zeb, and Mr. David and Miss Laura, too." She shimmied down in the bed and tugged the covers to her neck. "I love y'all."

"We love you, too," Zeb answered, giving her another smile and patting the top of her hand. "We'll be back tomorrow night."

"Awesome," Faith whispered, her eyes growing heavy and another yawn slipping free.

Laura and David walked back down the hall passing murals of David and Goliath, Moses and the Ten Commandments, the Garden of Eden and then Noah's Ark again as they neared the elevator.

"Thank y'all for coming," Shea called from the nurses' station.

"We were glad to," Zeb said, and Laura and David nodded in agreement.

Laura waited until they were on the elevator and

the doors slid closed, then she said, "Bless their little hearts."

Zeb nodded. "I feel the same way. This means a lot to them, to have people care enough to visit and spend time with them on a regular basis."

"It meant a lot to us, too," David said. He stood next to Laura in the elevator, and she felt his hand slide against her palm, then his fingers clasp with hers. The motion was sweet, tender, like the precious moments they just spent together with those children.

"I needed someone to help me out here," Zeb said. "I couldn't spend enough time with the group and also with Faith, or any of the others when they're unable to leave their rooms. Tonight, having your help meant the world to me."

"You can count on us, anytime," David said.

The elevator door opened at the first-floor lobby and they stepped out, with Zeb stopping a moment to look at them. "That's what I was just thinking," he said. "I *can* count on you." He took a step in the opposite direction. "I'm going to say hello to the lady that runs the flower shop before I leave."

"You want us to wait on you?" Laura asked.

"Nah, y'all go on home. I know you and those babies need your rest." He nodded his goodbye and then walked away.

Laura and David started out of the hospital, and he said what she felt.

"That was one of the most rewarding things I'v
ever done." He let go of her hand to open the doo
for her as they exited the hospital, and Laura imme
diately missed the contact of his skin against hers.

"I can't believe I've never thought to visit the kid
on the children's floor before," she said. "Readin
to them was incredible. They were so into the stor
and so appreciative of us coming to see them. I'n
looking forward to coming back tomorrow."

"Me, too." He opened the passenger's door of hi
car.

Laura slid into the seat and then waited for hin
to shut the door, but he didn't. "Everything okay?
she asked.

David leaned into the car, took the seat belt an
gently draped it across her and then snapped it int
place, his face so close to hers she could smell a hin
of peppermint on his breath. "You're amazing," h
said. "You know that?"

Embarrassed, she felt her cheeks blush. "Yo
really think so?"

"I know so." He still leaned into the car, so clos
that Laura would merely have to move forward
couple of inches to have her lips touch his.

She could feel her heart beating solidly in he
chest as she waited for...whatever he planned to dc

"Remember when I told you that you'd know if
took you on a date?" he asked.

She blinked. "Was this a date?"

His smile broke free. "No, this is me, asking you for a date, tomorrow night after we visit the kids here. So, Laura, would you like to go out with me, on an official date, tomorrow night?"

She didn't hesitate, and she didn't let her promise to herself not to get in another relationship hinder her words. This was David, a completely different kind of guy than she'd ever gone out with before, a guy who'd been there for her when she needed him most, and a guy who made her feel something so special that she didn't want to miss the chance to see exactly where the feelings would lead. "I'd love to."

"That's what I was hoping you'd say." He slowly eased out of the car, shut her door, rounded the front and climbed in the driver's seat. Then he started the engine but didn't back up.

She glanced behind them and didn't see anything blocking his path. "Everything okay?" she asked again.

He turned to face her. "No, everything isn't."

"What's wrong?"

"I'm thinking that the whole time we're on our date tomorrow night we're going to keep wondering about something, and that wondering is probably going to make it where we can't enjoy our date," he said smoothly.

"Wondering about what?"

He smiled, leaned closer. "This." Laura hadn't been kissed in eight months, and she wasn't all that sure she remembered how, but David certainly did. His mouth was soft and inviting, teasing her lips and every last one of her senses.

When he pulled away, he must have been satisfied with the awestruck look on her face because he gave her a confident smile and said, "Now we won't have to wonder."

But Laura was already wondering…how long she'd have to wait to experience another kiss like that again.

Chapter Fourteen

David couldn't be happier with his choice of locations for their first date. The food at Messina's was amazing, as evidenced by Laura humming her contentment with nearly every bite. He pinched his lips together to keep from laughing, and she noticed.

"I'm doing it again," she said, shrugging. "I don't think I ever made noises when I ate before I got pregnant." She picked up another bite of lasagna with her fork and grinned. "But I also don't remember enjoying eating quite this much before."

"Personally, I think it's cute," he said. "In fact, I think several things you do fall into the 'cute' category."

She paused her fork in midair and then slowly placed it back on the plate, one corner of her mouth lifting as she turned all of her attention to David. "Several things?"

He nodded, enjoying the flirtatious banter of their first date. "Several."

"You realize you can't make a statement like that without elaborating," she challenged. "So…what things?"

"What things do you do that I find cute?" he asked.

The other side of her mouth joined the first to give him a full smile. "Yes. Tell me."

"Okay." He wasted no time with his list. "The way your eyes glisten when you talk about your baby girls. The way you glance away at the bookstore when you catch me looking at you. The way your voice softens when you read to the kids in the book club, and the way I know that it'll do the same thing one day when you read to your little girls. And the way the base of your neck blushes when you're embarrassed, or flattered, or whatever it is that you are…right now."

Her hand touched that small pink spot at her neck, and she looked down at her plate. "You sure do notice a lot, don't you?"

"When I find something interesting."

She lifted her eyes back to his. "You find me interesting?"

"I always have."

"I've always found you interesting, too." She cleared her throat, and David thought for a moment that she'd say more, but then she pushed her plate away. "I'm done. Actually, I think I was done three bites ago, but it was too good to stop."

He understood that they'd gotten a little more personal than she'd planned for their first date. But he was satisfied, sensing that they were growing closer, step by step. He finished off the last of his own lasagna and nodded. "Agreed, but I kept going, too."

"It is that good, isn't it?" the waitress said, nearing the table with a tray of assorted desserts. "We have our famous tiramisu, pignoli nut pie and cassata."

"Oh, I can't hold another bite," Laura said, "but those do look amazing."

"They are," the woman said.

"We'll take a tiramisu to go." David handed his credit card to her. Then to Laura he said, "You know you'll want it later."

She laughed. "Didn't take you long to figure that out."

The waitress nodded her approval then left the table to tally their check and get their dessert. A few minutes later she returned with the tiramisu boxed and bagged, David's card and receipt.

Laura started to stand, and David hurried to get up and help her out of her chair.

"I'm attempting to be a gentleman here."

"And I'm getting more and more used to having one around," she admitted. She leaned into him as they left the restaurant, the two of them admiring the elegant décor and also saying hello to a few people they recognized from town.

When they neared the exit, David opened the door and a blast of cold air pushed inside.

"Oh, my." Laura turned her head away from the chilly wind.

David pulled the door shut. "Wait here. I'll go get the car."

She nodded. "I'm not going to argue with you."

Laura watched through the window as David walked across the parking lot toward his car.

"Excuse me."

She turned toward the man. She'd seen him before at church but didn't remember ever being introduced. "Hello."

"I'm Milton Stott," he said. "David's accountant for the bookstore. You're the lady he hired, aren't you?"

Laura nodded. "I am. I love working there." She glanced out the window and saw that someone had stopped David in the parking lot to talk, but she couldn't identify the man. She wished David would hurry. Milton seemed harmless enough, but he was definitely crowding into her three feet of personal space.

Then she realized why. He wanted to tell her something in private. His voice wasn't a whisper but just louder than one.

"I'm not trying to interfere in another person's business," he said softly, "but when I saw you tonight, I couldn't live with myself if I didn't warn you. A woman in your condition and all."

Laura turned her attention to the man. "Warn me? Warn me about what?"

"The bookstore," he said. "I'm assuming you're, well, relying on it as your source of income?"

She blinked. "Yes, I am." That was all she had for income until something came through at one of the school systems, which she didn't see happening before next fall. Then it hit her; this was David's accountant. He knew the true financial state of David's business. Laura had suspected that it wasn't doing well when she first arrived, but lately things had seemed so much better. "We've been doing very well," she said, in case the guy hadn't checked the books in a while.

"I'm sorry, miss." He shook his head, opened his mouth as though he were going to say something else, then stopped and pointed out the window. "Your ride is here." And this time it was a whisper, then he returned to his table in the dining room.

Even though the man hadn't directly said anything about the stability of David's business, he'd certainly implied that things weren't going well. And if anyone would know, it'd be the accountant, right? Laura felt like she'd been kicked in the stomach. What else could she do if things didn't work out at the bookstore? Especially after she had the babies?

She stepped into the cold, and the wind made her eyes water and drip. Or that's what she would tell David, if he asked. Because now the fairy tale she'd begun to see was starting to disintegrate before her eyes.

David hopped out of the car and moved to open the door. "I've got another surprise for tonight," he said. "I can't wait to take you..."

She forced a smile. "David, it's been such a long day, with work and then visiting the kids at the hospital and all. Would you mind taking me on home?"

David didn't know what had happened, but from the moment he'd helped Laura in the car at the restaurant, her disposition had turned a one-eighty. She'd been laughing, even flirty, throughout dinner, and now she stared out the window and didn't say a single word during the entire drive to her apartment. He parked the car by the rear entrance to Carter Photography. "You want to share the tiramisu before we end the night? That would at least put a little something special at the end of the date. I'd planned to take you to see the Christmas lights at Hydrangea Park, but tiramisu will do."

She'd finally turned her attention away from the window, and David was fairly certain she'd passed her hand across her cheeks before facing him. Was she crying? A few rapid blinks and a forced smile told him she had been, and he couldn't fathom why.

"Hey, what's going on?" he asked. "I thought our date was going well. Did I do something, say something wrong?"

She shook her head and did that rapid-blink thing again to ward off her burgeoning tears. "Tonight," she said, her voice raspy and raw, "was one of the best nights of my life. You didn't do anything wrong. You haven't done anything wrong at all, from the first day I came to Claremont." Then she sighed and added, "You've never done anything wrong toward me, from the time that we first met at UT. In fact, everything you've ever done has been," she sniffed, bit her lower lip and then finally said, "perfect."

"Okay..." he said, confused beyond measure. "Then why are you so upset?"

"The pregnancy hormones, they make me emotional."

"That's it? Because you seemed to be really enjoying yourself at the restaurant." He'd noticed her sensitivity over the past few weeks, the way she bonded so intensely with the children and the way she'd worried about her parents. However, he'd never seen her emotions change this quickly, and he suspected there was a reason. But he had no clue what it was.

"David, I..." She hesitated. "I need to ask you something, and I want you to tell me the truth."

As if he'd ever give her anything less than the truth. "Anything."

"You'll tell me the truth, even if you don't think I want to hear it?"

He'd always told Laura the truth, even when she didn't want to hear it, like in college when he told her Jared wasn't right for her. Back then she didn't listen, but now, he could tell that she would. "I can't imagine what you don't already know, but yes, I'll tell you the truth. I promise."

"You always have," she said, reiterating David's very thoughts.

"So ask me what you need to know," he said.

"The bookstore. Is it not doing well? And are you paying me when you can't afford it?"

Her questions blindsided him. He ran his hand through his hair, his jaw tensing as he instantly dreaded giving her the truth this time. "Why are you asking?"

"Your accountant was at the restaurant tonight," she said. "He came to talk to me when you went to get the car, and he hinted that things weren't going well at the bookstore…at all."

David was floored. He hadn't seen Milton at Messina's, but the restaurant by nature had several dimly lit areas to provide the customers with privacy. But this time, it'd given his accountant a chance to hide…until he apparently found a chance to speak to Laura alone. "What did he say, exactly?"

"He said he felt like he should warn me, and he asked if I was relying on the bookstore as a source of income. I think he was trying to help me."

"Milton had no right." David plunged his hand through his hair again then moved his fingers down to his neck and pushed against the tension spreading like wildfire.

"I'm sorry if I upset you," she said.

"You didn't. He did."

She fidgeted with the strap of her purse. "Is it true?"

"The bookstore has been doing better than ever since you came. I've told you that, and I meant it," he said, keeping his voice calm in spite of his anger toward his accountant. He didn't want Laura feeling as though she'd done anything wrong by asking about the state of his business. Because of her, David thought he might actually make it into the black again by spring. "It's been amazing since you've put your touch on the place."

Laura lifted her brows and tilted her head as though waiting for the "but" that she knew was coming. And in order to tell her the truth, David had to say it.

"*But* the problem is, it hasn't been doing that good for the past couple of years, ever since I inherited it. Or truthfully, it'd started going down years before. People are moving into the ebook market, and a lot of folks stopped shopping at a brick-and-mortar store. Or that's what I'd thought. It turned out, they just needed the place to offer events of interest, get books they wanted to read and promote them. Everything you've been doing. If I'd have started that two years ago, everything would be different now."

"You're saying that our recent sales aren't enough, though," she said.

"You shouldn't be worried about any of this," David said. "And Milton may have just lost himself a client."

"I really think he was only trying to help, David," she said. "And I've..." She took an audible breath. "I've decided what I'm going to do."

"What do you mean, what you're going to do?" David feared what she was about to offer, for her to stop working at the bookstore, because that was the exact opposite of what needed to happen. He *needed* her there. More than that, he *wanted* her there. "You don't need to do or change anything. You just need to keep helping me make it happen. We can do it together, Laura."

He'd just started thinking that there could be something between them, more than friendship, more than a boss-employee relationship. This had been their first date! And, because of Milton, it'd gone from perfect to the perfect storm. Because he could see it in her eyes. Laura had made up her mind.

"You can run the things at the store on your own, and I can eliminate all of the expenses associated with my employment. Besides, I wasn't going to be able to keep coming in during those weeks after I have the babies, and honestly, I still didn't know how I was going to afford to put them in day care whenever I could start back to work," she said, telling him exactly what he didn't want to hear.

"I told you..." he said.

She interrupted him. "I know you said I could bring them to the bookstore, but there's really no place there for babies, and I can't do that to you." Another deep breath, and then she set her thoughts free. "I'm going back to Nashville, to my parents' home. Everything is going to be more settled there now that my dad has finally figured out what's been bothering Mom all these years. And they're happy to support me until I get a teaching job somewhere."

"Laura, that's not what you need to do," he said, but she opened the car door and started out without waiting for David to help her this time.

"I'm sorry, David. I'm going home." And then she closed the door to the car...and slammed the door of his heart.

Chapter Fifteen

Laura should've called her mother last night, but she didn't feel like talking about everything and only wanted to cry herself to sleep, which she did. Reluctantly, she dialed the number this morning. The phone rang once, twice and then Marjorie picked up.

"Laura, how are you, dear!"

Laura moved the phone away from her ear to make sure she dialed the right number. Her mother always had a polite greeting, but today she was practically singing. Sure enough, the display showed she'd dialed *Mom*.

"I'm—" she didn't want to lie to her mom "—I've been better."

"Oh, honey, what's wrong? Is it the babies? I can come right now. Early labor? What are you feeling? Have you called the doctor?"

Laura should've thought about how close she was to her delivery date, merely a month away, before she said she wasn't doing well. "It isn't anything physically, Mom."

"Aw, bless your heart. It's David?"

Over the past weeks, her mother had insisted that Laura had feelings for David. Laura never denied it, but she didn't specify the extent of those feelings before. Today, however, she would.

"I think I may love him."

Her mother got silent on the other end and for a second, Laura thought she'd lost the connection. Then her mother's sigh echoed through the line. "Oh, honey, that's wonderful. I'd been so afraid that your heart was so torn by Jared that you wouldn't be able to fall in love again, at least not for quite a while. This, well, like I said, it's wonderful. Does he feel the same?"

"I don't know. I think he may feel the beginnings of something because he asked me out on a date."

"When are you going out?" her mother asked.

"We went out, last night," Laura said, and before her mother had a chance to start celebrating, she added quickly, "and it didn't end well."

"Wh-what? How did it not end well? What do you mean?"

"I'm fairly certain that he took me in as a charity case. The bookstore has apparently had some rough years, and it doesn't look like he's going to catch up. I don't think he can afford to pay me. In fact, I don't

think he's ever been able to afford it, but he's bee
doing it anyway."

"The bookstore seemed to be doing well when
was there," her mother said, "and your father sai
it was packed on Black Friday."

"It is doing well now," Laura said, "but his ac
countant hinted that it happened too late. And fror
the way David acted when I asked him how the busi
ness was doing, I'm afraid it's true." She'd walke
to the kitchen while they were talking then opene
the refrigerator and stood there. Nothing looked ap
pealing, and she thought she knew why. She didn
want to go back to Nashville, but she also didn
want to hurt David in any way. "Mom, I'm comin
back home."

"Here? To Nashville?"

"Yes. It's still okay for me to stay with y'all, isn
it? Until I have the babies and then find a job?"

Laura waited, and when her mother didn't readil
answer, she asked again, "Mom? It is okay, right?

"Well, yes," her mother said. "Or, it woul
be-e…" She drew the word out. "I was going to wa
and surprise you with our news, but now I'm nc
sure how we'd surprise you. We thought you love
Claremont and would be there for Christmas, an
then stay there when the babies are born. We wer
kind of counting on it."

"Counting on it?" Laura asked, closing the refrig
erator door. "What does that mean?"

"I guess I'll start with the first part of our news," her mother said. "I quit!"

"You quit what? Your job?"

"Yes, after twenty-one years of service, I left. Told them just last night. And I am so surprised at how great it feels to retire!" She paused. "Can you call it retiring if you're only forty? Anyway, whatever it is, I did it, and I'm thrilled!"

Laura was floored. Her mother quit work? "I'm glad you're happy, Mom, but why did you quit?"

"And that's the second part of our news. Your dad," she giggled, "it sounds so funny to say this, but your daddy asked me to marry him again! I know you saw the ring and all—he told me you were with him when he picked it out. But you should've seen the proposal. He took me to the Opryland Hotel night before last and got down on one knee right there in the middle by that big fountain. Then he announced to everyone that he loved me and wanted to spend the rest of his life with me." She laughed. "Can you believe that, Laura?"

"Yes, but I thought he was going to wait until Christmas. He told me to keep the secret."

"That's the rest of our news. I quit because we want to enjoy each other more, and we want to enjoy those grandbabies we're about to have. So I was planning to come to Claremont for Christmas and stay there to help you until the babies came and then also stay after they were born for a while. If I don't have a job, I can do that. And your dad went ahead and asked me so I'd know his plans, and then I could decide whether I wanted to quit work and spend all of the holidays with you in Claremont. And—this is the best part—we're going to renew our vows at the little community church there that you said you love so much!"

"Here? In Claremont?"

"Yes. Your father called and reserved the church this morning. It's going to be extremely small, with the preacher there, Brother Henry I believe was his name, and you as my maid of honor and then David as the best man."

"David?" Laura's head spun. "Dad is asking *David* to be the best man?"

"It seemed only natural, since we're having the ceremony in Claremont. Your dad has some good friends here, but none that want to travel to Claremont for us to renew our vows on Christmas. Everyone spends Christmas with family, and we're going to spend it with you."

"And David." Laura didn't plan to stay here more than long enough to pack her things. She couldn't be here at Christmas. She couldn't continue hurting David's business—or David, period—by sticking around. And she couldn't help but wonder if this wasn't the best thing anyway, her leaving town and severing this "relationship" or whatever it was with him before it really got started. His business was struggling, and he loved that bookstore, and he didn't need a dependent—a woman who was about to have two dependents of her own, no less. Talk about baggage.

"Honestly, when your dad mentioned him, I thought it'd be a great idea, since you two have been getting so close. Your dad is going to call him this morning. He may already have called, in fact. And you did say you think you may love him."

"I also said I'm hurting him financially, and I have no way to fix that. David—" she swallowed "—he deserves so much." Way more than she had to offer. Laura plopped down at the kitchen table and shook her head. What would she do now? "I can't let him take me in like a charity case."

"You aren't a charity case." David's voice came from behind her, and Laura whirled around to see he'd entered the kitchen from the front of the store.

"Oh, is that David? Tell him I said hello," Marjorie said.

"Mom says hi," she said miserably. This phone call was supposed to cement her return home; instead, it seemed her mother wasn't interested in doing anything but coming here. "I'm not going to stay and cause you to go further in the hole. I'm going home."

"Oh, Laura, do you really think..." her mother began, but Laura cut her off.

"I'll call you back later, Mom. I have to go." She

disconnected and looked at the tall gorgeous man invading her kitchen. "How did you get in?"

"It's ten o'clock. Mandy opens the front door at ten, and I was waiting for her when she arrived. You're supposed to be arriving at the bookstore now, by the way." He smirked. "You're late."

"I just need to get my coffee mug," Mandy said, entering the kitchen. She stopped in her tracks when she took a look at Laura. "Oh, uh, are you not working today?"

"No." Laura then remembered looking in the mirror before she'd started down the stairs. Her hair was sticking out like a troll doll, and she'd been so upset last night that she hadn't taken time to match her pajama top to her pants. Consequently, her hot pink and neon green plaid maternity pajama pants clashed severely with her oversize Vols orange nightshirt and purple slippers. But Laura didn't care. She wasn't going to work, and she didn't invite David over. He could take her the way she came, which was messy. And fairly gross. Maybe this would convince him that he didn't want to keep her around after all.

"Yes, she's coming to work," David said, deflating that idea, "if I have to drag her there."

"You wouldn't dare," Laura challenged.

"You think just because you're a little pregnant that I couldn't toss you over my shoulder and haul you down the street if I wanted?"

Mandy's laugh came out with force, and Laura shot her a look that promptly shut her up.

"S-sorry, Laura," she said. "But the thought of you, as pregnant as you are, being hauled down the street on his shoulder..."

"It's not happening," Laura said.

Mandy looked to David as if wanting affirmation.

"I'm not hauling her anywhere, especially when she's dressed like that," he said.

"Hey!" Laura snapped, and Mandy laughed again, then grabbed her coffee mug and retreated to the gallery.

"I need you to work," he said, "at least until Christmas."

"David, your accountant insinuated that you didn't need to hire me, you don't need to pay me. If I went back home, that would help you. You can still do everything without me."

"No, I can't. I need someone to run the *Boxcar Children* book clubs. I need someone to lead the women in their discussion this week about Rahab. They don't want to listen to me do it, and you know you're enjoying those meetings. Plus, there are the kids at the hospital. They look forward to you reading to them."

"You could do that," she said.

"Not like you. Are you really going to let them down? Could you live with yourself if you let Faith down? She looks forward to our visits each week, and she'll ask why you aren't with us. Seems to me she's gotten even more attached to you, probably since you're female, or maybe it's because you're having the babies. But in any case, I can tell Faith really likes you and enjoys your visits. *I'm* not going to tell her that you aren't coming back. If you're going to Nashville, you'll have to be the one to tell her."

"You know I can't do that. I can't hurt her."

"But you can hurt me?"

"I am hurting you, your business, every day I stay."

"We've still got the holiday season. You never know what could happen at Christmas," he said. "What if we sold enough for me to catch up on my line of credit and even see the bookstore make a profit? What if we could make it work…together? There is a possibility, but there isn't if I have to do it all on my own."

"Milton Stott didn't think so," she reminded.

"Then that's what we'll pray for."

She grabbed an apple from the bowl of fruit on the table, rolled it between her palms as she thought about his suggestion. "You want me to stay until Christmas."

"I do. And you really should anyway. It'd be a shame for you to miss your parents' wedding."

She cut her eyes at him. "Daddy already called you?"

"I'm the best man. Of course he called." He sat

beside her at the table smiling as though he'd won first prize at the fair, then he reached for the apple in her hand, brought it to his mouth and took a bite.

"That's mine," she said.

"Say you'll come to work, and I'll give it back."

She glared at the apple. She hadn't really been all that hungry for it before, but now that David was teasing her, she wanted it. Now. "Just until Christmas. I don't want to let the kids down."

He handed her the apple. "That'll work," he said, "for now. And get dressed. You're late."

Laura chomped a big bite of the apple, and he laughed, then turned and left the kitchen.

Chapter Sixteen

"I brought a Barbie for my book buddy." Savannah Jameson placed her wrapped gift beneath the Christmas tree in the children's area. "Daddy and I picked the one wearing a pink dress, since Faith's favorite color is pink. And I made her a pink card, too, with a snowman on it."

"She's going to love that, Savannah." Laura had been so excited about her idea to pair the kids at the hospital with the book-club children for Christmas. Each child that came to book club received the name and information about one of the children in the hospital and was told they could give their "book buddy" something for Christmas. It could be something they made, like a card or a poster, or a bought present. So far, each child brought both, something handmade and something purchased. She couldn't wait to deliver the gifts later tonight with David and Zeb.

"I got Timmy some Hot Wheels cars," Kaden said, sticking his gift under the tree, "and I drew him a cool car picture, too, that looks like one of the cars in the pack."

"He'll love that, Kaden." Laura waited for all of the children to place their gifts under the tree and then opened the *Boxcar Children* book. But before she said anything about the book, she stared at the tree, her mouth falling open. "Hey, did any of you put all of those candy canes on the Christmas tree?"

Their answers came back in a flurry of excitement, because everyone in town knew what candy canes meant.

"I didn't," one said.

"Nope!" yelled Kaden.

"Wow, he was here!" Savannah gasped then placed her hand over her broad smile.

Laura held up her palms. "Now, wait a minute. Let me ask Mr. David." She leaned out from the group and called toward the counter, where David was busily checking out customers. "David, did you put all of these candy canes on the tree?"

"Candy canes?" he answered, the same way he'd answered every other night when Laura had done the very same thing with the previous book-club meetings. "No, I didn't put candy canes on the tree."

"Well, I guess someone left them there for all of you," she said, and the kids scurried to the tree and grabbed their candy canes from Secret Santa. Their eyes were alive with wonder as they ate the candy, particularly since Christmas was merely three days away.

Laura smiled and began reading, and as soon as David had finished with the customers, he came over to listen and gave her a thumbs-up for pulling off the candy-cane scene again. She'd put the candy canes on the tree because she loved the idea of Secret Santa and wanted to help whoever it was keep his secret. Laura wasn't alone. Over the past few weeks, candy canes had shown up everywhere. On each table at Nelson's. On each photo in Mandy's shop. On the doors of each store. Under the windshields of parked cars. The entire town got in on trying to protect Secret Santa's identity, or maybe they just enjoyed getting in on the fun, but Laura loved every minute of it, especially bringing the fun to her book clubs.

When the book club had finished, Zeb showed up ready to ride with them to the hospital. The older man hadn't been feeling well and had started taking David up on his offer to drive him each night instead of Zeb taking his own vehicle. But Mr. Zeb wouldn't miss the trips to the hospital, especially tonight's visit, when the children were having their Christmas party and they'd distribute the presents from their book buddies.

Laura started toward the tree to gather the presents, but Zeb stopped her.

"Now, hold on, Miss Laura. You're going to have to stop lifting things. Those babies look like they're getting mighty close to an arrival, and we don't want you to overdo it and give them any reason to make an early appearance," Zeb said, stepping past her to pick up the gifts.

David laughed. "I'm trying to watch her, but she tends to do what she wants." He picked up the large bag he'd already started filling with gifts and joined Zeb at the tree to add the rest to the sack.

Laura placed a hand on her stomach. "I have to admit, getting up and down is becoming more and more difficult. But they aren't kicking anymore. Every now and then, they'll shift a little, but no more kicks."

"That's probably because they've run out of room," David said.

Laura pinched his bicep. "Very funny." She and David had grown so close over the past few weeks, and she couldn't imagine leaving in merely a few days. Being with him simply felt "right," and she didn't want to be away from him, definitely didn't want to leave.

But she would. She had to. She couldn't stay in Claremont as David's charity case, and she knew David would never leave his beloved town. He'd told her about his grandmother's farmhouse and indicated he'd live there one day. He hadn't added "with his family," but it'd definitely been implied. Laura would have her own family soon, and even if she had to live with her folks for a while until she found a teaching job, she'd eventually find a way to support herself and her babies. And in the meantime, David would probably realize that one of the pretty single ladies in Claremont would be a perfect companion for him for life. A woman who wasn't such a burden. That's what he deserved. Not an unemployed single mother of twins.

"Ready to go?" David asked, snapping her out of her silent pity party.

"Sure."

David carried the oversize bag filled with gifts down the hallway on the children's floor, anticipating the moment he finally got to see the kids. He and Laura enjoyed their time together at the bookstore each day, but nothing beat the moment when the day ended and they came to the hospital. She'd attempted to keep her distance from him over the past few weeks, reminding him every so often that she'd need to leave after the holiday, but even so, these nightly visits to the hospital were so special for both of them that they'd ended up growing even closer because of the love they'd developed together for these kids.

And, whether Laura admitted it to herself or not, David thought she had also felt the connection between the two of them. As though they were one.

He'd held his tongue when it came to telling her how he felt because he wanted to wait until the sales numbers came through from the Christmas season and then show her that the bookstore would be okay…and the two of them had no reason not to pursue a life together. According to Milton, the books looked "a little better," but still weren't going to put him in the black anytime soon.

However, David's hope for a relationship with Laura was now on the line, and one way or another, he would convince her to stay in Claremont. He just didn't know how.

Swallowing past the lump in his throat, he nodded to Shea Farmer and the other nurses. "They ready for us?" he asked.

She laughed at the bag David had borrowed from Mr. Feazell, the owner of the Tiny Tots Treasure Box. Red velvet and lined with white fur, it qualified as a real Santa sack. "They're going to love that!"

"That's the goal," he said. "And what about the hats?" He'd purchased three Santa hats from Mr. Feazell, and he, Laura and Zeb each wore one.

Shea gave him the okay sign. "Perfect."

As they walked down the hall, Laura started laughing.

"What is it?" David asked.

She pointed to her stomach. "We should've rented an entire Santa suit. I could've pulled it off without any stuffing."

"You'd be the cutest Santa around," he said.

"I'll second that," Zeb agreed as they heard the Christmas music blaring ahead.

"We let them turn it up loud tonight, since they're all in the playroom," Shea said. She and a few of the other nurses were following them to the party.

"Even Faith?" Laura asked.

"She didn't want to miss the party, and she's having a good day. A good month, really. Her parents haven't told her yet, but they think she may get to go home for Christmas."

David's steps faltered, and he looked to Laura. Her hand had moved to her heart. That was exactly what they'd been praying for. "That's wonderful," he said.

Faith had been in the hospital longer than any of the other kids, and David got the impression that her parents hadn't been certain she'd be able to go home again. But she was.

Thank You, God.

"Mr. David! Miss Laura! Mr. Zeb!" The kids yelled their names as they entered, big smiles on every face. Their parents were also here for the event, and they lined the walls taking photos with their phones and cameras as the trio entered.

"I'm going to miss them so much," Laura whispered, almost so quietly that it wouldn't be heard. But David did hear.

Please God, help me figure out a way to keep her here.

He got a grip on his emotions and smiled at the kids. “Well, hello. Guess what. Your book buddies sent each of you Christmas presents!”

The clapping and cheering consumed the room as David, Laura and Zeb handed out the gifts. Along with the nurses, they helped the kids open their presents, each child thrilled with the gifts from their new friends.

David spoke to each of the kids, but he spent a little extra time with Faith before the party ended. “You look like you’re feeling better today,” he said.

“I am,” she said. “I’m so glad I got to come be with everybody at the party. This was great, wasn’t it?”

“Yes, it was.”

“Did you see my candy cane? Secret Santa brought them for all of us.” She held up a candy cane. “Isn’t that neat?”

“Very neat,” David said, smiling toward Shea, who he assumed bestowed the candy canes on the kids.

“Okay, everyone, we’re going to need to get you all back to your rooms,” Shea announced, “but don’t worry. We’ll have another party tomorrow when the church comes to visit, and then another one on Christmas day.”

The kids cheered. “Lots of parties!”

Shea laughed. "That's right. This is party central, right here."

Zeb, Laura and David stood at the doorway to tell each child good-night as they headed out. Since the parents were in attendance, most of the kids were taken back to their rooms by their folks, and all but a couple of the nurses followed Zeb, Laura and David down the hallway as they left.

"Did you give them the candy canes?" David asked Shea.

"We've been doing that, too, at the bookstore," Laura said. "The kids love it, don't they?"

Shea nodded. "They do love it, but I didn't do it. The candy canes were delivered with a note asking us to give every child a candy cane from Secret Santa." She smiled. "He does that every year. And one of my friends that works at the nursing home says he sends them to every patient there, too, and all the nurses." She pointed to the nurses' station. "He sent them to us, too. That's mine, by my computer. I plan on snacking on it later," she said, "and thinking about Secret Santa, of course."

"That's wonderful," Laura said.

"I know."

As they started to turn toward the elevator and Shea returned to the nurses' station, she said, "David, can I see you for a moment?"

"Sure," he said.

"We'll go on to the elevator and wait for you," Zeb said.

"Okay." David followed Shea to her desk. "Everything all right?"

"Yes. I'm just following orders."

"Orders?"

She nodded, then glanced toward the elevator where Zeb and Laura were talking about the kids. "I am supposed to give these to all of you from Secret Santa. That's what his note said. But the note said this letter is for you only and that you're supposed to read it in private." She handed three candy canes and a small envelope to David.

Bewildered, he looked at the envelope, and sure enough, his name was written on the outside. He didn't recognize the handwriting, but the block letters would've made that practically impossible. "Thanks." He looked up to see Laura had turned toward him, and he held up the candy canes with one hand, while he slid the letter in his pocket with the other.

She smiled. "For us?"

"For us." Then to Shea, he said, "Thanks."

"You're welcome. I don't know what it is, but it was fun to help him out."

David didn't know what it was, either, and he looked forward to the moment when he got home and found out what Secret Santa had to say.

Chapter Seventeen

David read the note as soon as he returned home then had a difficult time sleeping, anxious to follow through with Secret Santa's instructions. The next morning, he woke early, ate breakfast and then waited for Laura to arrive.

She came in looking wistful, last night's cheer gone. "Those kids—they're amazing, aren't they?" she asked, obviously unable to get the children from the hospital off of her mind. But instead of looking happy about what they'd accomplished, providing a Christmas party and gifts for the kids, she looked miserable.

"They are amazing," he agreed and waited to see if she'd explain what had happened between last night and this morning to change her outlook.

She glanced around the bookstore, empty as usual for the morning. Thankfully it'd been filling up as each day progressed, but the mornings often reminded him of the fact that the place had been empty for several years before it'd been steadily filled. "You've done a lot of good here. I hate to think about it closing," she said.

"I do, too," he said. Milton had delivered updated financial reports on Monday, and this time David had shared them with Laura. On Tuesday, they agreed that he shouldn't borrow any more money from his line of credit and risk losing the farmhouse. He would close the doors December 31 and attempt to find another job in Claremont. He'd already been looking unofficially but had come up with nothing. If he had something lined up, maybe he could convince Laura to stay, to let him support her until she found a teaching job. Because the thought of Laura leaving didn't sit well, at all. And it was about time for him to tell her why.

"Laura, I don't want you to—" His words were cut short when the bell on the door sounded.

Zeb, wearing the Santa hat from last night, slowly entered.

"What were you saying?" she whispered.

David didn't want an audience for this conversation. "I'll tell you later."

"Still feeling good about those kids," Zeb said. "That was a great party, wasn't it?"

"Yes, it was," Laura said.

He started to smile but winced midway through.

"You feeling okay, Zeb?" David asked.

"For my age, if I get out of bed and can move around a bit, I'm feeling okay," the older man answered. "I'm heading over to the nursing home this morning and wanted to take a few more of those suspense novels for Miss Tilly. Can y'all help me get a few together?"

"I've got to leave for a few minutes," David said, "but Laura will help you out."

She reached for his forearm, and he wished his long sleeves didn't keep her skin from touching his. They'd kept everything low-key, done their jobs and been friends, ever since that date night. But David wanted to feel that closeness again. He wanted to hold her, and to kiss her, and to tell her how he felt—that he'd fallen in love with her—and then he wanted to tell her that she should stay in Claremont, and somehow they'd work everything out.

"You'll tell me whatever you were going to say?" she asked. "Later?"

David nodded. "Definitely."

For the first time this morning, she gave him a soft smile, and David prayed that everything would be all right. Somehow. But before he could work out the details, he needed to find out more about the note from Secret Santa. "I'll be back in a little while, and then we'll talk."

"Getting more building supplies?" she asked. "What are you building up there, anyway?"

"Nah, I finished up with my apartment last week, and it was just a little renovating," he said. Actually, it was a lot of renovating, and it appeared all of his work was in vain. The new room would probably never be used.

He ran a finger over the note in his pocket. "I'm going to the coffee shop," he said. "Y'all want anything?"

"Already had three cups," Zeb said. "And I won't be here but a few minutes. Just going to pick up the books and then head on. Brother Henry offered to drive me to the nursing home this morning, and we're leaving soon."

"Okay, how about you, Laura?"

"Oh, yes, a mocha latte please."

"You've got it." He left the bookstore and made a mental note to go by the coffee shop after he followed the instructions on the note.

Waving to Laura and Zeb as he left, he did a double take to make sure she'd turned her attention to locating the older man's books and didn't watch where he headed. When they disappeared toward the rear of the store, David walked purposefully down the street and stopped in front of Claremont Jewelry before reading the note again.

Tomorrow morning, go to Claremont Jewelry.
Tell Marvin Grier I sent you. S.S.

"Okay, Santa, here goes," David said, opening the door and walking inside.

Mr. Grier was at the checkout counter ringing up the only customer in the store, Chad Martin. "Every year I've tried to surprise Jessica with her present, and every year she finds out before Christmas." Chad accepted the small bag from the man then pointed a warning finger to David. "You tell her you saw me in here, and I'll tell Laura the same."

"Oh, I'm not shopping," David clarified, even though he'd love to be able to shop for Laura in this store—would love to buy a ring that she'd wear for life, a ring that would proclaim she loved him as much as he loved her, truth be told. But that wasn't why he was here. "I just came in to see Mr. Grier."

"Sure you did," Chad said, grinning. "Don't worry, I'll keep your secret...but don't you forget to keep mine. Just two days until Christmas. Maybe I'll actually pull off the surprise this year."

"Maybe so," David said, tired of trying to explain why he was here, which was impossible, since he had no idea.

But Mr. Grier did. The minute Chad exited and the door snapped shut, he said, "I've been expecting you, David."

"You have?"

He nodded. "Each year, Secret Santa typically purchases one or two things from me. I'll find an envelope with cash and instructions by the register, and I never see who puts it there. Same thing every year. And this year, I got an envelope with instructions for you."

"For me? I mean, I like your store and all, but I don't really need any jewelry."

"Obviously Secret Santa thought you did." Mr. Grier handed David a small box and an envelope with his name written in the same block letters.

David opened the envelope and read…

This is not a gift. I am repaying a debt. S.S.

He ran a thumb over the top of the black velvet box then lifted the lid.

"No way."

The ring was stunning, three diamonds centering an elegant band. Exactly the type he'd buy for Laura, if he could.

"Laura tried that one on," Mr. Grier said.

"She did?" David was shocked.

"When her father was looking for the new wedding set for her mother," he explained. "It fits, by the way, in case you're wondering."

"But I can't accept this. And he says it's repayment for a debt? No one owes me anything."

"Well, Secret Santa must think he does because that's a beautiful ring, and it's paid for." He looked behind the counter. "Hold on a minute. Yes, here are the appraisal papers for it. You'll want that for insurance."

David flipped through the papers, saw the value of the ring and gasped. "Definitely no one owes me that much!"

"You'll have to take that up with Secret Santa," Mr. Grier said, "assuming you figure out who he is." He smiled. "I'm guessing you won't." Then he looked at the ring. "And I'm guessing you might be getting yourself a fiancée for Christmas. I really like Laura, you know."

"I really like her, too." David lifted the ring out of the box and held it up to the light. It was amazing.

"The three diamonds are princess cut," Mr. Grier explained, "and they represent the past, present and future of your love."

"And it's paid for," David said, finding it hard to believe.

"Paid for and yours."

He folded the appraisal papers and slid them into his back pocket. Then he put the ring box in his front right pocket. Maybe this was a sign—a sign that everything would work out. Somehow he'd find a way to make a living in Claremont…and keep Laura here, too. As his wife, if she said yes. "Thank you, Mr. Grier," he said, leaving the jewelry store in a state of disbelief. He, David Presley, had an engagement ring in his pocket…and a woman he wanted to give it to.

"Don't thank me," Mr. Grier called, "thank Santa."

Chapter Eighteen

David had started back to the bookstore but then remembered he was supposed to get coffee and backtracked across the square. Funny how a diamond ring in his pocket made him forget pretty much everything else. He opened the door to The Grind and was met by the warmth of the fireplace filling the room along with the crisp scent of coffee coupled with the sweet scent of fresh baked cookies.

"Merry Christmas Eve Eve," Rhonda said as he entered. Several people from town sat on the sofas and at the tables spaced sporadically around the coffeehouse and most all of them waved a hand or fingertips to David.

"Merry Christmas Eve Eve to you, too," he said, feeling as chipper as she looked in her green-and-red sequined Christmas cap and matching Christmas ornament earrings.

"There's a table open by the fireplace," she said, "or do you want something to go?"

"Two mocha lattes to go," he said.

She smiled knowingly as she jotted down the order. "For you and Laura?"

"Yes," he said, already liking the ring of that. David and Laura. It sounded really good. Felt even better.

"Want cookies, too? We made iced sugar cookies today."

"Why not? Give me four."

"All righty. They're shaped like Christmas trees, wreaths, stockings and snowmen. You have a preference for which ones you get?"

"One of each," he said, looking forward to watching Laura enjoy the treat. In college, he never saw her eat sweets; however, her pregnancy had her craving a bit of sugar almost every day. David was happy to oblige, just to see her smile. He really liked seeing her smile.

Rhonda moved behind the pastry counter and started getting David's cookies while the barista prepared the lattes. The band More Than This played Christmas music beside a decorated tree on one side of the shop, and David enjoyed the songs so much that he nearly didn't hear Rhonda's comment.

"So, was that Laura's brother looking for her earlier?" she asked. "I sent him over to the bookstore to find her."

David turned away from the band to look at the

waitress. "Laura's brother?" He shook his head. "Laura's an only child. Someone was looking for her?"

She checked the white sack to see the cookies she'd already placed inside and then reached for a snowman one to add to the bag. "Yeah, not long ago. I know I've never seen him before. I'd have remembered. He kind of favored her, so I thought he might be her brother. You know, blond, nice features," she said, and she blushed. "Tall. I was actually going to ask if her brother was moving here, maybe." She slid a stocking cookie in the bag and then folded the top down. "And, you know, whether he was single?"

Obviously Rhonda had taken a quick interest in whoever this guy was, a tall, nice-looking blond dude who wasn't from around here and was looking for Laura. His old roommate's image came to mind.

"He, um, had the greenest eyes I've ever seen," she said. "Maybe that'll help you figure out who it is? You know anybody like that?"

I think the first thing that caught my attention was his eyes. And it's still so hard for me to look at his eyes and not just melt. Laura's confession from college, on a night when she'd been hurt by Jared's flirting with one of her friends, had clued David in on the effect of his buddy's unique eyes on women.

Obviously, Rhonda wasn't immune.

"You know who he is?" she asked, and David realized she'd been scrutinizing his response to every tidbit of information she revealed.

"I think I do." And he wondered why Jared had come here, to Claremont. "Was anyone with him?" Like, say, his wife?

"No," she said. "He was by himself. And he said he needed to find Laura as soon as possible because he'd made a terrible mistake and he wanted to fix it. I figured it was one of those sibling arguments, you know, like me and my brother have. Figured he came here to apologize in person. He seemed like the kind of guy that would do that," she said dreamily.

Great. Yet another one taken with Jared. And Jared, apparently, was currently with Laura.

"So…is he single?" Rhonda asked, sliding the sack of cookies across the glass counter toward the two white cups holding their lattes.

"No, he isn't," David said.

"Right," she answered disappointedly, while David took his coffees and cookies then headed toward the door…wondering if he'd just told a lie. Was Jared single now? Did the "mistake" he was talking about include leaving Laura, the mother of his twins, and marrying someone else? Would he have left Anita already and decided he had made a mistake, that he still loved Laura? That he should've married Laura?

The brisk December cold hit him even harder, an abrupt change from the warmth of the coffeehouse. Or maybe it merely felt colder because of the cold reality that the father of Laura's babies had come to town. The guy Laura had loved first.

He looked toward the bookstore and saw the door open. David took a step back to stand beneath the coffeehouse's awning and prayed that the two wouldn't look his way. He didn't want to talk to Jared, but he wanted to see—no, he didn't want to, but he needed to see—him interact with Laura. Did she still want him?

Sure enough, Jared stepped outside with Laura standing within the open door. David watched as his old friend reached out and ran the backs of his fingers along her cheek. He saw Laura turn her head into Jared's touch.

David couldn't watch anymore. Jared was here, and he obviously wanted her back. And from all appearances, Laura wanted him, too. Well, of course she did. This was the guy she'd loved throughout college, and this was the father of her babies. They *should* be together. David felt a sharp stab of pity for Anita, the woman Jared had apparently married on a whim and then dumped to be with the woman… he never should have left.

The woman David loved.

"Hey, Mr. David, did your friend find you?" Kaden asked, running down the sidewalk toward David.

"My friend?" David asked.

Kaden nodded exuberantly while Mandy, carrying Mia, tried to catch up with her son.

"Kaden, you need to slow down," she said breathlessly, and then to David, "your old roommate from college came into the bookstore while we were there. He asked where you were."

"Did he?" David glanced past Mandy to see Jared walking away from the bookstore, and from David's vantage, he appeared to be smiling. If he'd actually been interested in seeing David, he'd have stuck around until he returned, wouldn't he? But he hadn't. And David knew that was because he hadn't really been searching for his old roommate. He'd been looking for the girl he'd loved, the mother of his babies.

"Yeah," Kaden said, unaware of the tumult this conversation was inflicting on David, "but then he said he really wanted to just talk to Miss Laura, and then they started talking about her babies and stuff."

Mandy ran a hand across Kaden's curls. "That's enough, Kaden. We didn't mean to eavesdrop," she explained. "And we left so they could talk without an audience." She tilted her head toward Kaden.

David wondered what Jared had said that the boy had overheard.

"We aren't a audience," Kaden said with shrug. "Mr. David, is that guy her boyfriend?"

"Did he say he was?" David asked.

"Kinda."

David's skin bristled. "How do you mean?"

"'Cause he said he missed her and he hugged her and stuff, like if he was her boyfriend. Adam at my school has a girlfriend, but he doesn't hug her or anything. They just play on the monkey bars and the seesaw instead of Adam playing tag with us boys." Kaden shook his head. "I don't want a girlfriend 'cause I like to play tag."

David weeded through the information and zeroed in on what was important in his world. "He said he missed her."

Mandy nervously cleared her throat. "He mentioned that he'd missed Laura and that he had been thinking about her," she said. "But then we left."

"But remember? Miss Laura said she'd been thinking about him, too," Kaden added, unknowingly twisting the knife.

"Yes, I remember," Mandy admitted, her cheeks turning even more red. "And then we left." She gave David what she probably thought was a reassuring smile.

He didn't feel reassured. "Well, y'all have a good day." Turning away from the uncomfortable conversation, he reentered the coffeehouse and took a seat. More Than This started playing "Blue Christmas." David couldn't think of a more fitting song.

Laura couldn't believe how much had changed in the span of a few hours. Jared's offer was so heartfelt, so meaningful, so…unexpected. He wasn't the same guy that she'd known in the spring. This wasn't a man who would tell her to end a pregnancy. No, this guy already loved her babies because they were his, too. This guy had offered her a Nashville apartment to live in until she found a job. And he said he'd help her pay for everything, from now on, for the girls, even though Laura hadn't asked.

And all because he'd finally found faith…with Anita. His story had made Laura cry because now she understood. She'd found her faith again, too, because of David. But she'd been so touched listening to Jared describe how his eyes had been opened and how Anita had encouraged him to do what was right, especially since she was now pregnant, too. Jared and his new wife didn't want his twins not knowing the sibling they would have next summer.

Laura had promised to think about Jared's offer and consider it. Either way he would help her support the girls, whether she moved back to Nashville or stayed here. His offer would help her stay here… if that's what David wanted.

She prayed it was, that he would still want her in Claremont and with him even if the bookstore wasn't a factor. Because she knew she loved him. The thought of leaving him in two days had made her sick this morning, but now Jared had promised to help her out until she found a job. And she would find a job, eventually. No, it wouldn't be at the bookstore, but surely she could find something here to hold her over until she was able to get a position teaching at the school.

She simply needed David to tell her he wanted her to stay. And she suspected he'd been about to say that very thing this morning before they were interrupted by Zeb. Maybe he was even going to say more. The three words that she wanted to hear so desperately.

The bookstore door opened, and she turned to see David entering carrying two coffee cups and a small white bag. She smiled. "You just can't get coffee without cookies, can you?"

He didn't give her the smile she expected, but instead walked past her to place the items on the counter. "I guess not."

Laura started to tell him about Jared's visit and his offer, but there was something she wanted to cover first, something she hadn't stopped thinking about since he left. "You said you'd tell me what you were going to say this morning," she reminded, grabbing her mocha latte and taking a delicious sip. "So…tell." And then she'd tell him her news, too, that Jared would be helping financially.

David picked up his coffee, took a long sip and then swallowed.

Laura's skin tingled, she was so anxious. "So… what were you going to tell me? You said, 'Laura, I don't want you to…' and then Zeb walked in. You don't want me to—what?" She knew what he was going to say, that he didn't want her to leave. That he felt as strongly toward her as she felt toward him, and he wanted her to stay in Claremont and the two of them to work through everything together. Now and forever. She took another sip of her latte, let the rich mocha tease her tongue while she waited to hear him tell her how he felt.

"I don't want you to," he began again, then visibly swallowed and added, "stay in Claremont."

The coffee lodged in her throat and she forced herself to swallow it down. "Wh-what? You want me to leave?"

"The bookstore is closing. I tried to help you out, but I won't be able to anymore," he said, his words clipped and firm, without even a hint of compassion. "Your life is in Nashville. Mine is here." He took another sip of his coffee. "We're still friends, though," he added. "If you ever need me, and if I can help, I'll be here."

"Of course you will," she said, shaken by this change of events, "because that's what friends do, help you out when you need it…and then send you on your way." She waited for him to refute the statement, to tell her that wasn't what he was doing at all, but he nodded once, placed his coffee cup on the counter and then left her sitting alone.

Chapter Nineteen

David hadn't been able to find a way to back out of his commitment to be best man at this wedding. For the past two days, he'd only spoken to Laura when absolutely necessary, not wanting to make things even more awkward than they already were by trying to talk her out of leaving.

He'd told her to go, and after her parents said "I do," she'd do just that. Leave…and go back to Jared.

David had been shocked that she still hadn't even told him about Jared's visit, but then again, what good would telling him do? It wouldn't change the fact that Jared had shown up and now she was returning to Nashville, where she could be with the father of her babies.

David should be happy things worked out the way Laura wanted.

He *should* be.

Marjorie wore a fitted cream dress and carried

a bouquet of poinsettias. Thomas and David wore suits, as did Brother Henry. The only people present who weren't in the wedding party were Brother Henry's wife, Mary, who sat in the second row and dripped tears through the ceremony as though it were her own daughter getting married for the first time, and David's parents, thrilled to spend part of their holiday attending a vow renewal. None of them realized the pain he endured, attending a wedding with Laura present and knowing that the wedding he most wanted, the one between the two of them, would never happen.

"I just love this," Mary whispered repeatedly.

Several times, Marjorie, never taking her eyes from her husband, agreed, "I do, too."

But all of the others faded into the background for David. The only person he saw wore a pretty red dress and a smile that seemed forced. Laura had her hair pulled up and held in place with some decorative barrettes, a curled blond tendril hanging down on each side of her face. David wondered if she'd have worn her hair that way for *their* wedding day. Or if she'd wear it that way when she wed Jared.

He stuck his hand in his pocket, felt the ring Thomas had purchased for Marjorie and thought of the ring David had, courtesy of Secret Santa, in the opposite pocket. He hadn't wanted to leave it in his apartment. He hadn't wanted to leave it anywhere period. He'd wanted to put it on Laura's finger. And now that she was leaving, he should probably give it back.

But he had no idea who'd given it to him. The town was so protective of Secret Santa that David didn't have a clue to the guy's identity. How could he return the ring?

Laura gazed at her parents as they completed their vows, but as soon as they finished, she looked at David, her eyes filled with unanswered questions.

David couldn't look at her, so he focused on Thomas and Marjorie, finishing the ceremony with a kiss. Their show of affection went on a little too long for comfort, and Mary's tears turned to giggles. Brother Henry also chuckled, and Laura returned her attention to her parents.

"Sorry, but this is just so wonderful!" Marjorie gushed.

"I totally agree, Mom," Laura said. "It is wonderful. I'm so—" she brushed away a tear "—happy for both of you." Glancing at David, she frowned a little, then took a step toward her mom to hug her, and stopped. "Oh! Oh, my!" She grabbed at her stomach and winced.

"Laura, what is it?" Marjorie asked, while David rushed to her side.

"Laura? Is it the babies?" he asked.

Still wincing, she nodded, and David realized she was holding her breath. He forgot about the fact that they were barely speaking, forgot about the fact that his heart had been broken and solely concentrated on helping the woman he loved—whether she loved him back or not. "Breathe, honey. Hold on to me." He took her hands and she squeezed them nearly hard enough to break bone. Then she eased up, released her breath and said, "Not—not false labor."

"We'll go get the car and pull it around to the door," her father said, darting toward the church exit with his wife at his side. "David, you help her out."

Everyone in the church moved into action. Brother Henry and Mary rushed to open the doors as David guided Laura down the aisle and outside. His parents followed Laura's folks out so they could also head to the hospital. And David held his arm around Laura as she slowly progressed toward the vehicle.

Another hard contraction slammed her when they were merely feet from the car, and she latched on to David and yelled through the onslaught. It killed him to see her in so much pain, but what hurt even more were her words, directed to him in the midst of that horrible contraction.

As her faced flexed with pain, her arms clung to David and tears fell freely, Laura asked, "What—what happened to us?"

Marjorie, holding the back car door open for her daughter, locked eyes with David, her mouth flattening and her eyes suddenly filled with sorrow. Obviously she'd heard Laura's question, even though her daughter's yelp with yet another contraction kept David from having to answer.

He eased her into the backseat, and Marjorie slid in to sit beside her, draping her arm around Laura and still looking at David as though she didn't understand.

"I'll be right behind you," he said, closing the door without addressing Marjorie's questioning eyes. And without answering Laura's question.

Because he didn't understand, either.

Chapter Twenty

"They're beautiful," David's mother said, standing beside him at the nursery window while Grace and Joy slept peacefully in their pink blanket cocoons. Laura had said the names came easily after she went into labor in the church on Christmas day.

"They are, aren't they?" he agreed. The girls came two weeks early but were perfectly healthy. And now, merely two days old, they were doing great.

"What a Christmas present," she said.

"I couldn't have said it better myself," Zeb said as he neared the nursery. "How's the little mama?" he asked.

"She's amazing," David said. And she was. Laura had endured four hours of labor before delivering Grace and then three minutes later, Joy. Seeing her hold the baby girls, talk to them and love them over the past two days had touched David's heart like nothing he'd ever witnessed before and he wanted to tell her, but the timing had never been right. Someone was always in the room, and then on top of that, David kept wondering when Jared would show up to see his new daughters. If David were a smart man, he wouldn't stick around waiting for the inevitable, when another man waltzed in and claimed what he wanted so much. But David couldn't help himself; he wanted to be near Laura.

Zeb had been at the hospital several times over the past couple of days, not only to check on Laura but also to see all of the kids on the children's floor for Christmas. David had gone down to see them, as well, and had taken photos of the babies along. All of the kids had made cards for Laura, and they were displayed in her room. Zeb nudged David. "Whatever is going on between you two needs to be fixed."

"What?" David asked, but he knew exactly what the older man referred to.

"You and Miss Laura. You were meant to be together, and I think you know it. You two—" he pointed to the babies "—and those two." He nodded for emphasis. "Together."

"Zeb, you don't know what's happened," David said, and he didn't want to discuss the girls' daddy now, especially since Laura's parents were walking toward them.

"Laura still sleeping?" Marjorie asked as they joined David and Zeb at the window.

"I think so." David looked at the couple, their

arms around each other as if they were newlyweds. Then again, in a way, they were.

Marjorie held up a bag. "I've got a gift. Why don't you walk with me and we can go see if she's up? I think she's going to like this." She gave her husband a look that told David this "walk with me" thing was a setup. Obviously she wanted to talk to David alone, and all of the people huddled around the nursery window apparently knew it…and went along with it.

David looked again at the babies, their little mouths open as they slept with tiny fists near their lips. He'd been surprised Marjorie hadn't already asked him about Laura's comment on the way to the hospital, but again, the past two days had been a flurry of emotion with hardly any chances for private conversations. Until now. He prayed he was ready. "Okay."

They turned the corner and walked far enough away from the nursery that the group couldn't hear, and then Marjorie slowed her steps. "Laura is supposed to leave the hospital in an hour," she said.

"I know."

"Well, then, I think it's time we figure out where she's going, don't you?" She raised one intimidating brow to David.

"Where she's going?"

"Yes. Is she going home with us…or staying here with you?" Before David could respond, she added,

"She asked you what happened to the two of you, and from what I can tell, you still haven't given her an answer."

"I haven't had a chance to talk to her privately since we got here," David said, feeling like a kid who'd been called into the principal's office.

She handed over the gift. "Here. You can deliver my gift, and you can talk to her. Now. This is your chance. Because as much as I'd love for her to live with us, I refuse to drive her back to Nashville when I honestly believe her heart is—and will always be—in Claremont."

"What about Jared?" David knew he shouldn't have asked, but the question came out before he had a chance to filter his thoughts.

Now both brows popped up, her eyes widened and then she shook her head for good measure. "*That's* what this is about?" She gave him a small shove toward Laura's room. "Oh, you definitely need to go talk to my daughter. And in the future, that's the way the two of you should handle things. Talk things out. I went more than two decades keeping my thoughts and fears from Thomas. I was stupid. And you are, too, if you don't figure out what's what." Then she abruptly turned on her heel and started back toward the nursery.

While David, not knowing what was about to happen, continued toward Laura's room.

She was sitting up in the bed and smiling at her

phone when he entered, and David felt a sharp stab of jealousy wondering whether Jared had texted something that made her smile like that.

She glanced up and that confused look that had crossed her face every time she'd seen him since Jared came to town returned. Then she cleared her throat, turned the phone so he could see the image of the babies on the screen and said, "I love all of the pictures everyone has already put up of the girls."

David mentally kicked himself for, as Marjorie said, being stupid. He had to stop assuming things and start asking what he wanted to know. Starting right now. "They're beautiful." He held up the gift bag. "Your mom sent another gift."

Laura reached for the bag, and David handed it over, their fingers touching in the exchange. She hesitated as skin met skin, looked at him and then slowly took the gift. Peeking inside, she said, "These are the kind of pacifiers the nurse said the girls like best."

David nodded, his thoughts more focused on what he was about to say than on Marjorie's gift, and Laura seemed to understand. She placed the bag on the nightstand and then watched him pull a chair near the bed and sit down.

"So, are you going to tell me now?" she asked, her voice barely above a whisper, as though she also dreaded this conversation. "What happened?"

David hated seeing her upset because of him, but

the whole point of sending her to Nashville was to give her what she wanted and make certain she was happy. "I know how much you loved Jared, how you wanted him to marry you and the two of you to raise Grace and Joy together. And I know how much it hurt you when he didn't," he said.

"David..."

He shook his head. "Let me finish. I've held this in, and I should have told you when I saw the two of you together again."

"Oh, wait, David, you don't—"

"Laura, please," he said, and she stopped. David glanced at the door, still closed, and was thankful they finally had the privacy he needed to tell her everything in his heart. "I saw him leaving the bookstore and the way you looked at him. I could see that you love him, and I could also see that the two of you appeared to be working things out. Which is great. For the girls. I know that's what you want, and I won't stand in your way of that." He took a deep breath, let it out. "I just wish you'd have told me."

A different look came over her face, one David couldn't read, and then finally, she asked, "Why?"

"Why?" he repeated.

"Yes, why do you wish I'd have told you? Why would you care that Jared came to see me? And on top of that, why did you show up at the bookstore, barely speak to me and treat me as though you couldn't stand to look at me ever since? Why?"

When he didn't readily answer, she persisted, "You said you've held it in ever since that day. You didn't tell me what you wanted to say, what I believe you were about to say that morning before you left. Why?"

David had no choice but to answer. "Because I couldn't stand to see him with you."

She blinked. And the fire that'd been in her eyes merely a second ago converted to a warmth as she looked at him. Then she seemed to fight a smile as she asked once more, "Why?"

David decided he might as well go for broke. He'd already started down the rabbit hole, might as well fall in. "Because I know you love him, Laura, and I wanted..."

"You wanted what?" She reached for his hand and tenderly laced her fingers between his. "What is it that you wanted, David?"

"I wanted you to love me."

Her eyes glistened, and several tears fell free. "Oh, David," she said. "I will always care for Jared because he's the girls' father. But his life is with Anita, and with the baby she's carrying."

"With the baby she's carrying?"

Laura nodded, her tears still falling, but her smile sending them in awkward paths along her cheeks and neck. "That's why he came, to tell me that he's changed and that he wants to be a part of the girls' lives. He wants to help financially, too, and he said he'll help me out until I can find a job. And a lot o the change in him was due to Anita. She was deter mined to help him regain his faith, and he's tryin to get his life right. He wants to help support th babies and be a part of their lives."

David felt like an idiot. If he'd only asked, this i what she'd have told him. "Aw, man. I thought tha you wanted him again."

Her smile crept up a little higher, and she blinke through the tears. "I have one more question," sh said, her thumb moving in tender circles across th top of his hand as she spoke.

"Anything," he said. "I promise I'll answer."

"You said you wanted me to love you." Her eye locked with his, and the compassion David saw al most moved him to tears, as well. "Why?"

He didn't have to think about his answer. He gav her the truth. "Because of how much I love you."

She eased forward in the bed, moved her fac toward his and said, "I do love you, David. I lov you so much that it killed me to think about leavin you. I don't want to leave Claremont. I don't wan to leave you. Ever."

Their last kiss had been timid, tender and sweet But this one held the intensity of the emotion pass ing between them, the promise of a future together the eagerness of beginning their life together an loving each other forever.

"Now that's more like it," Marjorie said, enterin

the room with a smile stretching into both cheeks and with Shea Farmer following in her wake.

"Well, I take a couple of days off, and you go and get the whole hospital excited about the beautiful twins on the fourth floor." Shea held up a small paper red sack. "I did want to come up and see you and the babies, but I also needed to bring this. I'm not sure when it was left at the nurses' station, but apparently, I've turned into something of an honorary elf for Secret Santa. He left this with a note asking me to deliver this to you."

"Deliver what?" Marjorie asked.

"A candy cane for David and Laura, but you aren't supposed to open it until you leave the hospital," Shea said. "Wait..." She pulled a note out of her scrubs pocket and read it. "He said you're supposed to read it after you leave the hospital but before you go home."

"O-kay," David said.

"I've got to get back down to the children's floor," Shea continued. "I'm glad I got to see all of you, and I'm very happy about the girls."

"Us, too," Laura said.

Shea had been gone only a few minutes when a different nurse came in. "Laura, your little ladies will be ready to go in about five minutes. We're sending for a wheelchair for you now."

"Wonderful." She waited for the nurse to leave. "I wish I could have had a little more time to get the apartment ready. Mandy said she still had the cradles from when she and Mia were babies and would let me borrow them, but I haven't even put them in my room yet. They're still in one of her storage areas." She looked at David. "I am staying here, aren't I?"

"If you can forgive me for being a horse's behind," he said, which earned a tiny snort of a laugh from Marjorie.

"I think I can," she said.

"And if you can live with the fact that I'm currently unemployed with no prospects whatsoever of a job."

Marjorie emitted another laugh, but Laura reached for his hand. "We'll sell the bookstore together, and we'll find something for us to do together. I want to stay here, David. I want to be with you."

Ten minutes later, all of Laura's and the babies' things were in the trunk, Grace and Joy were buckled into their infant carriers in the backseat and David helped Laura into the passenger's seat. While everyone hovered around the car oohing and aahing over the scene and snapping photos right and left, David hovered over Laura to buckle her in and to steal a tender kiss.

She loved him, and she wanted to stay in Claremont. It'd be the perfect opportunity for him to give her the ring he still carried in his pocket…but he still didn't know how he'd support a wife. And he couldn't ask her to marry him without being able to take care of her. So he said a silent thank-you to God for giving him a beginning to the life he wanted, and he said another prayer for God to help them complete the story.

Then he circled the car, got in and prepared to drive her home. But Laura pointed to the candy cane sticking out of David's shirt pocket. "Ready to read it?"

He nodded and withdrew it while the rest of their families headed to their cars so they could apparently get to the apartment before them and make sure the place was ready for the new arrivals.

"Go on, I can hardly wait," she said, placing her hands together at her mouth as David peeled back the paper around the stem and silently read the note.

"I don't get it."

"What does it say?" She leaned over to see. "We're supposed to go to that address?"

He nodded, dumbfounded. "I guess so."

"Do you know where that is?"

"I know exactly where it is, and I…really don't understand."

Chapter Twenty-One

It took fifteen minutes for David to drive to the address Secret Santa provided. He turned down the familiar gravel pathway that he'd traveled often growing up but hadn't seen in several months.

"Are those peach trees lining the road?" Laura asked.

"This is actually a driveway," he said, "and yes, they are. The peaches are some of the best you'll ever taste, too. I used to eat so many when I was little that my folks were afraid I'd get sick."

"You've been here before?"

David pulled past the last trees lining the drive and then viewed the open fields that bordered the white farmhouse and red barn. "I own it," he said, blinking to make sure his eyes weren't playing tricks on him. But they weren't. The barn had a fresh coat of paint, as did the white fencing. But the barn and the fencing had nothing on the house. "That's my grandmother's house. My house now," he said. "But the last time I saw it, the windows were boarded, and the house needed painting badly."

"That's your house? David, it's beautiful! It looks like something out of a magazine."

He'd dreamed of seeing the house look like this again. "I don't understand how..." He stopped as a man exited the front door—the new red front door—and waved.

"Isn't that Savannah's daddy?" Laura asked.

David pulled the car up to park beneath the big oak in front of the house. "Yes, it is." He got out as Titus Jameson walked to meet them.

"Hey," he said. "That's perfect timing. I just finished." He looked into the backseat. "Oh, wow, they're as pretty as I heard. Congratulations."

"Thank you," Laura said, also exiting the car but slowly.

David glanced her way. "Honey, you okay?"

She nodded. "Yes, I'm fine. That wheelchair was hospital policy, so I put up with it, but they've been having me walk for the past two days. I'm good to go."

David smiled at her determination. He loved that about her, loved everything about her, in fact. "Okay," he said, and then turned to the guy standing by the car. "Titus, what—well, what are you doing here?" he asked, opening the door to the backseat and unhooking Grace's infant carrier so he could carry her inside.

Laura opened the other door for Joy, but Titus intervened. "Here, that'll be heavy for you to get with the seat and all," he said, and then he proceeded to unhook Joy's carrier.

"I figured you already knew why I was here," Titus said as they walked toward the house. "But I really wasn't sure how he did it all—Secret Santa, I mean. Remember when I came in the bookstore not knowing what I was going to do about work and Christmas for Savannah? Well, the next day I got an envelope of cash and a credit at the building supply store with instructions to fix this place up for you. So that's what I've been doing," Titus said with a grin. "He's left me notes every now and then about things he wanted done, and when I got a note—on a candy cane, of course—I did what it said."

"Seems like everybody does," Laura said, crossing the porch and putting her hand on the door. "Can we go in?"

"Of course," Titus said.

Laura opened the door and then held it wide so Titus and David could carry the babies in. They placed the carriers on the hardwood floor near the stairs, while David stood in awe. The walls had all been painted the original shade of creamy yellow, and the furniture that had previously been covered with sheets had been recovered with new fabrics in shades of rust and gold that gave the place a homey, farm appeal.

"I could so live here," Laura whispered.

Titus winked at David. "Listen, Daniel and Mandy are watching Savannah for me, and I want to spend some time with her today, so I'm going to head on out. Everything is done here. This morning was the last finishing touches. I'm going to leave so you can have some privacy to see your new home."

David nodded as Titus saw himself out, and then he simply moved through the place to appreciate the beauty of the restored home. "It's exactly like I dreamed," he said. Then he heard Laura's gasp and turned to see what had her attention.

She faced the fireplace in the living room and stood with her mouth open as she focused on the photograph above the mantel.

"I never saw the photo," David said, staring at the picture, "but I remember when Mandy took it."

Laura blinked several times as she took in the image of herself, reading to the children's book club, Savannah leaning against her and peering at the book and Kaden peeking at the page. Several other children faced her and leaned forward to hear every word. "That touches my heart," she said.

"Mine, too."

The front door opened, and David turned, expecting to see that Titus had forgotten something, but instead Zeb walked in.

He'd started moving slower lately, and today was no exception. "Okay if I come on in?"

"Of course," David said, walking to welcome their guest. "How did you know we were here?"

"Titus," he said, smiling as he moved to the stairs, held the rail and then sat down beside the carriers. "They're so beautiful."

"Thank you," Laura said.

"I..." Zeb began, then reached out to touch Grace's tiny hand. "I have something to tell both of you, before the others arrive."

"Others?" Laura asked. She walked over and sat on a cushioned chair near the stairs. David moved to sit beside her and held her hand.

Zeb nodded. "I believe a few folks are in on this little secret, or they will be soon."

"Because of Titus?" she asked.

"Because of Secret Santa." Zeb looked up at them and smiled. "All of those years that you've been giving me those books for free," he said to David, "I kept up."

"You kept up with what?" David asked, confused.

"With what I owed. I kept up with my debt," Zeb said. "I had a debt to repay. That's the thing about helping others, about giving to others. God gives you back so much more. All these years I've been visiting the hospitals and the shut-ins and the nursing homes, I've gotten close to a lot of folks, lots of times during their last years, their last days." He sighed, apparently reflecting on some of the people he'd helped over the years. "I give them my time." He shrugged. "I give them God's love."

David concentrated on listening to everything Zeb had to say.

"And when it comes their time to meet their Lord," Zeb continued, "they leave the stuff that doesn't matter up there to me, 'cause they know I'll give it to the ones who need it, and I do. To the best of my ability, I do."

"Oh, Zeb." Laura reached for his hand.

"It's you, isn't it? You're Secret Santa," David said.

Zeb nodded. "I am."

"I can't thank you enough," David said.

"I'm just doing what's right." Zeb looked at the sleeping babies. "This place was meant for the four of you."

"Oh, Zeb, we aren't—I mean, David hasn't asked me," Laura stammered, but David merely grinned at the older man.

"No, I haven't, but I've learned something over the past few days. When you've got something to say, or in this case, something to ask, then you certainly shouldn't waste time."

Zeb grinned, and Laura's mouth dropped open.

"David?" she asked as he moved in front of her and lowered to one knee.

"Laura, I've loved you for longer than I was willing to admit, but I'll never make that mistake again. If I'm thinking that I love you, I'll say it. If I want to hold your hand, I'll hold it. If I want to kiss you and love you and cherish you for the rest of my life—and I do—I promise I'll do it." He slid his hand into his pocket and withdrew the ring that'd been keeping him company for the past five days.

Laura gasped as he opened the box. "That's—that's my ring!"

"If you'll say yes, it is," David agreed.

"Yes, yes, oh, yes!" she said as David slid the ring on her finger and marveled at the beauty of the three sparkling stones, even prettier on the hand of the woman he loved.

"For our past, our present and our future," he said.

"Maybe you can have a Valentine's Day wedding," Zeb said, "so I can be there to see it?"

David didn't like the way that sounded, at all, and from the way Laura tensed, she heard the same thing. "Zeb, what are you saying?" David asked.

The older man took another glance at Grace and Joy then wiped a couple of tears away. "I've been waiting a long time to be with my Dolly again. And now, according to the doctors, I don't have to wait much longer. Three months at the most, they say." He turned his attention from the babies to Laura and David. "That's why Valentine's Day might work."

Laura's tears were flowing now, and she took

Zeb's hand in hers. "Valentine's Day would be perfect, especially if we have you there."

David nodded, unable to speak for the emotion squeezing his heart.

"I want you two to run the bookstore the way you have, taking care of the children in town and also those special ones at the hospitals and the nursing homes. And, Laura, I know you wanted to teach at a school, but what you do at the bookstore, that's important teaching, too. And at the hospital. I truly believe you were meant for those things."

David believed so, too, and he wanted the bookstore to stay open and for her to be able to continue working with children there, but even with a place to live, he wasn't sure…

"David," Zeb continued, breaking into David's thoughts.

"Yes?"

"Your bookstore is going to be fine now."

David was floored. What was Zeb saying? "Going to be fine now?" he asked.

Zeb nodded. "The line of credit on the farmhouse is taken care of, and as of this morning, you're debt-free."

"Zeb!" Laura exclaimed, and David shook his head. "It's—gone? Paid for? All of it?"

"All of it," Zeb said with a nod.

"I— Zeb, I don't know what to say."

"You should tell your fiancée about her Christmas present, the one from you, since she'll be able to use it now," Zeb said.

David hadn't even mentioned the gift to Laura, since he had thought they wouldn't get to use it, but he swallowed, cleared his throat and said, "The work that my dad and I did over Thanksgiving upstairs, and that I've been pecking away at ever since..."

"Yes?" Laura asked.

"We finished a room for the girls, a place for them to stay when we're at the bookstore. Thanks to my dad's help, it turned out very nice. I think you'll like it."

"I've seen it," Zeb said. "It's beautiful."

"Oh, David, thank you." She hugged him tightly and held on. "And, Zeb, thank you so much for giving us this gift!"

"Zeb," David said, "I don't know how we can ever repay you."

Zeb's mouth slid into a smile. "I do. Say you two will take over, when I'm gone on to see my Lord and be with my Dolly."

"Take over," David repeated.

"You need a new Secret Santa," Laura said, obviously putting the puzzle together quicker than David.

"I believe I need two, if you get right down to it," Zeb said. "It's been a lot for one person to handle, but I've been watching you over the past months, the love you have for children, for the community and for each other. That's what I was looking for, what I prayed for, and God gave it to me…with you." He reached in his back pocket and pulled out a tiny black bank book. "This here will tell you what I have in the account for your giving. Actually, what you have, since I've already added your names to the account. And this is how it works. The more you give, the more you'll have in the account. I know it doesn't make sense, but that's the way God does things." He smiled. "Trust me."

David took the book. "We do, Zeb. We do."

The sound of crunching gravel alerted them that someone else had arrived.

"That will be all of your family and friends," Zeb said.

"How did they know to come here?" Laura asked.

"That's easy. Candy canes."

Epilogue

Laura hadn't even realized her father was interested in changing schools until he announced he'd taken the eighth-grade teaching position vacated by Mr. Nance at Claremont Middle School. He transferred in January, so he and Marjorie were already settled into a house not far from the town square by the time Thomas had the blessed opportunity to walk his daughter down the aisle on Valentine's Day.

"Are you ready, honey?" he asked, patting Laura's hand.

Laura looked to the front of the church, where Brother Henry held his Bible and waited to perform the ceremony, and David stood waiting to make her his wife, to love, honor and cherish her as long as they both shall live.

Thank You, God, for this day, and for the man that I love. Thank You for our baby girls and for making my family whole again.

Grace began whimpering from her spot in Marjorie's arms, but Joy, as usual, slept away in the arms of her Papa Zeb.

Laura concentrated on every word of the ceremony, on every beautiful emotion pulsing through her being as she said her vows. And then David surprised her when he asked for Marjorie to bring Grace and Zeb to bring Joy and stand beside them.

Then Brother Henry continued, "David, repeat after me. With this ring, I thee wed."

David took Laura's hand and gently slid the ring on her finger. "With this ring, I thee wed."

In the rehearsal, this was the part where David kissed her, but instead of that happening now, Brother Henry spoke again.

"Because this marriage is so much more than the joining of two hearts but is instead the blending of four lives, David asked to also give a token of his love and devotion to their daughters."

While Laura watched in awe, David withdrew two small gold rings from his pocket and lovingly slid one on each girl's tiny finger. "I love you," David said, then looked to Laura. "All of you. You are my life, you are my love."

Brother Henry nodded. "And you may kiss your bride."

David took the woman he loved in his arms and replied, "Gladly."

* * * * *

Dear Reader,

Growing up, I remember my Paw-Paw picking tur
nip greens and leaving them in sacks on the porche
of those who he knew loved the leafy veggie. H
would deliver them early in the morning before the
woke and never told anyone of his gift. One woma
reciprocated by bringing Paw-Paw cakes and leav
ing them with my grandmother at the house whe
he was out in the field working. Neither said any
thing about the gifts. Over the years, I've hear
other stories of secret givers, but it's the Secret Sant
stories, the ones that happen in the season wher
we're thinking about God's gift of His Son, tha
touch my heart the most.

I enjoy mixing facts and fiction in my novels, an
you'll learn about some of the truths hidden withi
the story on my website, www.reneeandrews.com
While you're there, you can also enter contests fo
cool prizes. If you have prayer requests, there's
place to let me know on my site. I'll lift your reques
up to the Lord in prayer. I love to hear from read
ers, so please write to me at renee@reneeandrews
com. Find me on Facebook at www.Facebook.com
AuthorReneeAndrews. And follow me on Twitte
at www.Twitter.com/ReneeAndrews.

Blessings in Christ,

Renee Andrews

Questions for Discussion

1. Laura had two main reasons for leaving her home in Nashville. What were those reasons? Do you think leaving was her best option?

2. David found his dear friend asking for help when he didn't feel he had any help to offer, yet he helped anyway. Can you think of any biblical examples that follow this principle of giving even when you don't have much to give?

3. Zeb found his joy in helping others. Do you know anyone like this? Do you think that, like David, people often will go out of their way to help those who help others?

4. Marjorie's main issue throughout the beginning of the book is that she didn't feel wanted; she didn't feel she was chosen. How can we relate her feelings to the way we feel with or without God in our life?

5. Why do you think the entire town joined in on the distribution of Secret Santa's candy canes?

6. Laura told the book club children about the children in the hospital and helped form a bond between the healthy children and those who were sick. What do you think it teaches those chil-

dren, both the ones in the book club and the ones in the hospital?

7. Titus Jameson's little girl Savannah was withdrawn due to her mother's abandonment, yet she opened up to Laura. Do you know a child who has been hurt or disappointed by an adult? How can you reach out, like Laura did, to bring that child out of his or her shell?

8. Zeb looked forward to being reunited with his sweet Dolly. Do you know of anyone longing for heaven even more because of a loved one who's passed on? Zeb coped with his separation by keeping himself busy serving others. How do you or those you know cope with the separation?

9. In my life, I've heard of a few instances of real Secret Santas, providing gifts or financial assistance during the Christmas season without any acknowledgment or recognition. Do you know of any real Secret Santas? How do you think their presence impacts the recipient's life?

10. Did you see any symbolism in the names used in the book, specifically the children's names?

11. Many people have "family" members who aren't blood related, those who have grown as close as family over the years. Zeb was this type of in-

dividual in David's life, and then in Laura's. Do you have anyone like Zeb in your life? Or are you that person in someone else's life?

12. Laura's parents moved to Claremont to be closer to their daughter and granddaughters. How do you think having family nearby can benefit new parents? Do you see any ways that it might not be beneficial?

13. Brother Henry, Mary, Daniel, Mandy and all of the other "church people" that Laura met could have tried to make her feel guilty for turning away from God, but instead they showed her love and compassion, reminding her that God still loved and wanted her. How do you think she would have reacted if they'd tried to "guilt her" back to God?